CLAIMING
MY BRIDE OF
CONVENIENCE

CLAIMING MY BRIDE OF CONVENIENCE

KATE HEWITT

MILLS & BOON

First published in Great Britain 2019
by Mills & Boon, an imprint of HarperCollins*Publishers*
1 London Bridge Street, London, SE1 9GF

Large Print edition 2020

© 2019 Kate Hewitt

ISBN: 978-0-263-08414-6

MIX
Paper from
responsible sources
FSC™ C007454

This book is produced from independently certified
FSC™ paper to ensure responsible forest management. For
more information visit www.harpercollins.co.uk/green.

Printed and bound in Great Britain
by CPI Group (UK) Ltd, Croydon, CR0 4YY

CHAPTER ONE

TINKLING LAUGHTER FLOATED from the open doors of the ballroom, along with the expensive clink of the finest crystal. The party was in full, elegant swing, and it made my stomach cramp and my heart race. Could I really do this?

Yes, I could. I *had* to, because the alternative was to scuttle back home to staid safety and more years—potentially *many* more years—of living in stasis, waiting and wondering.

Admittedly in this moment I was sorely tempted to flee from this luxurious hotel in the most sophisticated square of Athens, back to the safety of Amanos. But, no. I'd come too far, was hoping for too much, to run away like a frightened child. I was a woman, after all—a *married* woman. And after three years of marriage I was finally confronting my husband—but first I had to find him.

I straightened my shoulders, smoothing my hands down the sides of the gown I'd purchased

that morning in one of Athens's upscale bou-
tiques. The sales assistants had exchanged laughing looks as I'd stammered through my request—I
had plenty of money but little knowledge when
it came to fashion or style, and they'd known,
and had made sure I had *known* they'd known,
as well.

Now I caught sight of my reflection in a gilt
mirror in the hotel lobby and wondered if the
tight ruby-red strapless gown was outrageous
or elegant. Did it even suit me, with my brown
hair, brown eyes? Miss Unremarkable, my husband once called me… Not that I blamed him for
it. He'd wanted an unremarkable wife, someone
who would make no splash, no demands, pres-
ent no inconvenience, and that's exactly what he
got…for three years. But now I wanted something else, something different, and I'd come
here to get it.

I took a shaky breath, willing my jelly-like
legs to move forward. I could do this; I'd got this
far, hadn't I? I'd taken a ferry from the remote
island paradise where I'd spent my entire married life, and then a taxi from Piraeus to Athens.
I'd booked myself into this very hotel, fumbling
with the credit card while the receptionist looked

on witheringly, and I'd managed to buy myself a dress and shoes—sky-high stilettos that made me wobble when I walked, but *still*.

I'd managed it all—even if it *had* taken what felt like all my strength, all my courage. Life on Amanos was so much simpler, and it had been a long time since I'd been in the city, with all its traffic and rudeness and noise. A long time since I'd faced my husband—a man I barely knew.

Matteo Dias—one of the richest, most ruthless men in Europe, as well as one of its most notorious playboys. And I was his wife.

It seemed incredible even now, despite the papers I'd signed, the vows I'd spoken. I'd woken up every morning for the last three years on an island paradise, far from the hopeless slog of my former life in New York City, and practically had to pinch myself. *Is this real?*

Until it hadn't felt like enough.

A flicker of apprehension rippled through me at the thought. Was I being unreasonable, greedy? *Stupid?* I had a lovely home, more money than I knew what to do with, and a fulfilling life— all of it more than I'd ever had growing up in Kentucky or during my brief, unfortunate stint in New York City. Could I really ask for more? Demand it, even?

Resolve hardened inside me and straightened my spine. Yes, I could. Because the alternative was to give up on the only real dream I'd ever had.

Now, as I scanned the crowded ballroom from its double doors, I wondered if I would even recognise my husband in the flesh. Of course I'd seen his photo in plenty of tabloids, almost always accompanied by some curvy blonde or other, usually simpering on his arm and poured into a dress.

I'd read all the speculation concerning his whispered-about marriage, with as many gossip columnists insisting no woman could have tamed him as those confirming the rumours were true, and Greece's most eligible bachelor was in fact secretly wed.

Of course they were both right. Matteo *was* married, but I hadn't tamed him. I haven't even spoken to him. All I knew about my husband of three years was what I'd read in the tabloids— that he was ruthless in ambition, amazing in bed, and highly desired by almost all women.

I'd studied his dark, closely cropped hair, those

cold steel-grey eyes, his impressive and dominating physique. I'd remembered how, for the brief moments we'd been together, it had felt as if he'd stolen the air from the room, how he'd just had to look at me and I'd forget to think.

I told myself that couldn't happen now, because I very much needed to have all my wits about me. But first I needed to find him.

'Miss, are you coming in?' A waiter, with a white cloth draped over one black-clad arm and holding a tray of glasses of champagne, raised his eyebrows at me enquiringly.

I swallowed hard. 'Yes,' I said, pitching my voice to sound as firm and bright as I could. I was afraid I sounded a bit manic. 'Yes, I am.'

With my shoulders thrown back and my chin tilted high, I stepped into the ballroom full of the cream of Europe's society. Barely anyone spared me a glance, and I was hardly surprised. I was a nobody, plucked from a dive of a diner in New York—a waitress with no pedigree, no breeding, no style or standing. Miss Unremarkable indeed.

Even in a gown that had cost an eye-watering amount—Matteo has always been generous with his money, if nothing else—and shoes that had cost more than a month's rent on my apartment once upon a time, I knew I looked the same. Dull-as-dishwater Daisy Campbell, born in the sticks of Kentucky, who hitched a ride to New York as a starry-eyed dreamer and soon wised up.

I moved through the crowds, keeping my chin up and my shoulders back with effort. Three years on a remote island hadn't accustomed me to this kind of scrutiny. Back on Amanos I had learned how to be confident. I was sure of my place there, because I'd made it myself. But here…everything felt different. *I* felt different— more like the nervous country-mouse-in-the-city I'd once been. I had to fight against the urge to ask someone if they needed a refill.

I needed to find Matteo as soon as I could, before I melted into a puddle of nerves or broke an ankle in these wretched shoes.

I wasn't under any illusion that he'd be thrilled to see me, but I was hoping he wouldn't be *too* put out. We'd had an agreement, and I was breaking it. But three years is a long time, and surely he couldn't have expected me to languish on Amanos for ever? Not that I was *languishing*, precisely, but I needed to move on with my life.

I'd given Matteo what he wanted. Now it was his turn to give me what I wanted.

'Good luck with that,' I muttered to myself, and someone turned to give me a hard stare.

I'd always had the slightly odd habit of talking to myself, and three years on a remote island hadn't helped matters. I gave the stranger a sunny smile and forced myself to move on.

Where was my husband?

Then I saw him and wondered how I hadn't before. He was in the centre of the room, the star of the show, standing half a head taller than any other man. My steps slowed and my heart started to beat hard. He was even more magnificent in the flesh than I remembered.

I stood there for a moment just watching him, because he was so beautiful. I didn't want him to be, because I knew that his cold, hard beauty would distract and unsettle me, and in fact it already was. Matteo Dias was breathtaking—a dark and powerful knight in his tuxedo, the expensive material stretching over his broad shoulders and showcasing his long legs and impressive chest. Even from across the room, I could see how his grey eyes glinted like silver, and his mobile mouth captured my fascination as he spoke.

We'd never kissed, barely even *touched*, and yet in that moment I was spellbound, caught by his sheer animal magnetism and intense charisma, as if we shared a physical history. As if I could actually remember the way he felt and even tasted, when I knew I couldn't.

I hadn't let myself even imagine either of those things, because our marriage had never been like that. Matteo had been clear on that point right from the beginning, his lip curling in derision at the thought of so much as touching me—and I'd told myself I didn't mind, because I didn't *want* to be touched.

I took a deep breath and started forward. 'Matteo.'

My voice came out more loudly than I'd meant it to, and several people turned. I heard whispers, titters, as their gazes raked over me. So the dress didn't work, then. I'd suspected as much, but I didn't care. Colour surged into my face but I kept my chin high, as I had all my life, no matter what it had thrown at me—and it had thrown a lot.

'*Matteo.*'

He turned, his eyes narrowing to silver slits as his lush mouth compressed into a narrow, unforgiving line. Clearly he wasn't pleased to see me.

I wasn't surprised, but stupidly I still managed to feel hurt, although I tried to hide it.

The woman by his side tilted her head towards him, her green cat's eyes glinting with malicious laughter as she whispered in a voice loud enough to carry, 'Oh, dear, Matteo, it looks like someone has a little crush on you.'

A *crush*? Hardly.

'We need to talk,' I told him, keeping my gaze focused on his now scowling face, refusing to be intimidated by the women who circled him as if they were a flock of elegant crows and he was their carrion. Except, of course, Matteo was all predator and no prey.

'Talk…?'

He pretended to look puzzled, and I realised he was going to try to act as if he didn't know me. The thought filled me with a sudden empowering fury. *No way, sucker.* Not after three whole years of doing what he'd said and staying out of his way.

'Yes, talk, Matteo.' I smiled sweetly even though inside I was trembling like a bowl full of jelly. 'You *do* remember who I am, don't you?' I forced my smile wider as I started to say the dreaded word. 'Your wi—'

'Not here.'

His hand clamped down on my arm and he steered me out of the ballroom as if I were an unruly member of staff. I tripped in my heels and Matteo steadied me, although I could tell the gesture was one of expediency rather than concern. My husband wasn't merely displeased to see me; he was furious.

That was made even more clear when he ushered me into a private room off the ballroom, closing the door behind him with a loud click.

'Daisy,' he said, his teeth gritted and his eyes flashing, 'what the *hell* are you doing here?'

I almost hadn't recognised her. Admittedly she was reassuringly easy to forget—which was why I'd married her in the first place. The only reason I remembered her name was because of the deposits I'd made into her bank account.

'Nice to see you, too,' she muttered, with a flash of spirit I hadn't expected.

Hadn't I married a mouse? A quiet, tame, unremarkable and *invisible* mouse, who was supposed to be grateful for what I'd done for her and stay entirely out of my way?

'We had an agreement,' I told her flatly.

'To keep me prisoner on an island while you gallivant about all of Europe?'

'What?' I stared at her incredulously. 'Is that seriously your version of events?'

'We're *married,* Matteo.'

My jaw dropped and I snapped it shut. I could not believe she was playing that card, when she of all people knew what our marriage really was. 'You signed the agreement, Daisy. You cashed the cheques. You told me it *suited* you.'

Her jaw was thrust out, her expression mutinous. I'd never seen her look so fiery—but then, of course, I'd barely seen her at all, and as they say, *out of sight, out of mind.* Entirely.

'I know I did, but it's been three years and I want something different now.'

'Oh, really?'

I folded my arms and stared her down. She had to be easy to intimidate. She certainly had been before—although in truth I hadn't even had to try. I'd offered her a deal—a generous, considerate, honest business deal—and she'd accepted. Clearly she needed reminding of those facts now.

'So you want something different and you decide to stalk me down to a public party—'

'I did not *stalk,*' she snapped, cutting across

me, which no one ever did. 'I read about the party online and decided to find you here.'

'I call that stalking.'

'Technically, I don't think you *can* stalk your husband.'

'Trust me, you can—especially in a marriage like ours.'

'Which is exactly what I want to discuss.'

She gave me an acidly sweet smile as she walked across the room—or rather minced, because that dress was so ridiculous—to sit in a chair, looking as demure as I could ever hope for, even though her eyes still sparked.

'What is that hideous dress you're wearing?' I asked, knowing I was being blunt to the point of rudeness and not caring in the slightest. 'You look like a tube of lipstick—and a nasty shade at that.'

Her cheeks flushed but her gaze didn't waver. 'I thought those snarky assistants at the boutique might be setting me up.'

'Couldn't you tell it didn't suit you?' Although, awful as it was, it *did* suit her. My gaze was reluctantly and irresistibly drawn to the slender curves the outrageously tight dress clung to. 'What *is* that material? *Pleather?*'

'I don't know.' She glanced down at it without much interest. 'They insisted it was the latest style, and who am I to know any different?'

'They were lying to you.'

For some reason it annoyed me that a couple of nasty shop assistants would make a mockery of my wife. Our marriage most certainly wasn't *like that,* but she was still a Dias. Even if no one knew it. Even if that was the way I'd wanted it.

'I thought they might have been,' she said with a shrug. 'I'm hardly a fashion icon, and I'm sure I seemed like a complete country bumpkin to them.'

Which begged the question—'What are you doing here, Daisy?'

Her eyes flashed. 'Don't you mean what the *hell* am I doing here?'

'I was surprised.'

I wasn't normally in the habit of justifying myself, and I didn't know what it was about her that caught me on the raw, made me defensive. That had to stop.

'Annoyed, you mean? Or perhaps furious?' One eyebrow arched as her golden-brown eyes glittered like bits of topaz. She was unremarkable, I told myself as I scanned her in cold assessment. Brown hair and eyes, a slight, un-prepossessing figure. Completely forgettable.

So why did I keep staring at her?

'We had an arrangement,' I stated, yet again. She seemed to need the reminder.

'Which suited you—'

'*And* you—to the tune of nearly two million euros.' I was not going to feel guilty. 'You knew the score all along. You said you were happy with it.'

Her lower lip—a surprisingly lush and rosy-red lip—jutted out, and she folded her arms across her slight bosom, which for some reason I was having the most exasperating trouble look-ing away from, considering how unimpressive it was. B cup at best, and yet…

'Well, now I want to change it,' she said.

I let out a short, sharp laugh. 'I don't negotiate.'

'Are you sure about that?' she challenged. 'It's hardly a binding contract.'

I stared at her, shocked. Where was all this bra-zen confidence coming from? And what could she possibly want from me?

'Not binding, no,' I agreed silkily, 'but you know the terms. If you wish the marriage to be annulled without my agreement, then you'll have to hand back every single euro you've received from me over the last three years.'

Which amounted to nearly two million—one million to start, and then two hundred and fifty thousand for every year she stayed married to me, until my grandfather died. Then we wouldn't have to have anything more to do with each other—something I had thought suited us both.

But of course Daisy knew the rules as well as I did. I'd outlined them all very clearly when I'd proposed to her after she'd been fired from a rundown dive of a diner in a less than salubrious neighbourhood in Manhattan and she'd accepted. With alacrity.

So what had changed?

I folded my arms and eyed her in consideration. She was sitting as prim as you please in a vamp's red dress, looking entirely incongruous and making me feel as if I didn't know her at all—which, of course, I didn't. I didn't need or want to know her. But I needed to know what she wanted.

'What is this really about, Daisy?'

For a second that confidence faltered. Her lips

trembled and her gaze slid away. 'What do you *think* it's about?'

'Why are you here? What is it you want? Because I really don't think you want to repay the two million euros I've already given you.'

'One million, seven hundred and fifty thousand,' she flashed back, recovering her spirit, assembling it like armour. 'And, according to our agreement, we were to be married for a maximum of two years. It's now been three.'

'And you've been paid accordingly.'

And she'd spent it all, judging by the amount in the bank account I'd set up for her. Last time I checked, its balance was hovering just above zero. Heaven only knew what she spent the money on.

'So what do you want?' I shook my head slowly, my lip starting to curl. 'More money?'

Her eyes widened, her lush lips parting. In that red dress she looked as ripe as an apple, ready to be plucked, and it disconcerted me. The last time I'd seen her she'd been in a drab waitress uniform, her hair scraped back into a ponytail, her face shiny with grease from the fried food she served. Hardly someone I'd ever think of *plucking*.

'Would you give me more money?' she asked, seeming more curious than greedy.

'No.'

I took a step back, away from temptation. As surprisingly luscious as Daisy seemed right now, she was most definitely off limits. The last thing I wanted to do was consummate—and thus complicate—my marriage. I had plenty of women to choose from. I didn't need this one.

'That's good, because I have enough money as it is.'

'You seem to spend it as fast as I can transfer it to your bank account,' I remarked sardonically. 'Although I can't imagine what you spend it on, living on an island with a population of about three hundred.'

'That's none of your business, is it?' Daisy countered.

She had a rather guilty look about her now, with a flushed face and sliding gaze. What *did* she spend the money on? Perhaps she'd redecorated my villa ten times over, or bought a boat, or a helicopter, or a closet full of designer clothes… Although, judging by that dress, it was probably not the last possibility.

'So what *is* it that you want, then?'

Impatience edged my voice and I made a point of glancing at my watch. Daisy Campbell—no, Dias—had taken up fifteen minutes of my valuable time, and that was fifteen minutes too many.

She cocked her head, her thick, darkly golden lashes lowered as she surveyed me, her lips slightly pursed. Was she trying to be coy? It was a surprising move, and one that unfortunately had the power to affect me.

Desire surged through my body in a white-hot rush, and although I was tempted to take another step back, to safety, I stood my ground. I would not be cowed by my unremarkable wife. Nor would I be affected.

'Well?'

'I'll tell you what I want.'

She stood up, as striking as a flame in that ridiculous red dress, her light brown hair tumbling about her shoulders, her face flushed, her chin angled at a determined tilt—the embodiment of both defiance and desire.

'I want an annulment. I want out of this sham of a marriage. And I'll give you all your money back to prove it.'

CHAPTER TWO

I WATCHED AS shock blazed across Matteo's features and stiffened his powerful body. Clearly he hadn't been expecting *that.* No doubt he thought I'd spent all the money he'd given me. If only he knew the truth...

'Why on earth would you want an annulment?' he blustered. 'What's the point?'

'That's none of your business,' I shot back.

The last thing I wanted was to expose my vulnerability to this man. I wanted out of this marriage because I wanted a chance at a real life, a real love, and I knew I wouldn't get it with Matteo Dias. That was a fact that sent a stupid pang through me, because even now, when he was being so irritatingly arrogant, part of me wished he'd notice me the way a man was meant to notice a woman.

Even in this tight red dress, I could see he was regarding me like something unfortunate he'd stepped in.

'It certainly is my business,' Matteo retorted. 'We're married, Daisy.'

'It's not a real marriage.'

'It is on paper.'

'I'm willing to pay back the money, Matteo. What objection can you possibly have?'

Except I'd known instinctively that he would object—that he was not the kind of man to let a woman dictate his terms. To let me be the first to walk away. And now, feeling the full force of Matteo Dias's ire was enough to have me trembling where I stood. Still, I was determined to stand my ground.

'I assure you I've thought this through very carefully. I would not be giving back one million, seven hundred fifty thousand euros lightly.'

'How on earth do you still have all that money?'

'What would I have spent it on?' I countered, which was not quite the truth.

'Seriously, Daisy…'

'I invested it,' I told him. 'And the profits will allow me to repay you and keep some for myself.'

He shook his head slowly, as if he couldn't believe I was clever enough to have done such a thing, or courageous enough to ask him for an annulment. But I was both, and I was proud of it.

His jaw hardened and he folded his arms. 'I don't wish to have an annulment.'

'That's too bad for you, then, isn't it?'

His eyes flashed dangerously. I knew I shouldn't have provoked him like that, but I wasn't having this high-handed manner now.

'Our agreement was clear, Matteo. I could have the marriage annulled at any time, as long as I gave the money back. You just never thought I would.'

His lips tightened. 'It is exceedingly inconvenient for me to have our marriage annulled.'

'Oh, dear,' I mocked. 'I'm *so* sorry.'

'*Don't*, Daisy.'

'How about *you* don't—don't stand in my way? I'm the one abiding by our agreement, Matteo, not you.'

Matteo shook his head slowly from side to side, as if trying to clear it. Then he shook it more forcefully.

'This is ridiculous. What on earth are you going to do once our marriage is annulled? Where will you go?'

'Actually, I intend to stay on Amanos.'

'What?' He stared at me in scathing disbelief. 'Not in *my* house.'

'No, of course not. I'll rent a place in the village.' I'd already seen one—a small, whitewashed one-bedroom cottage that was reasonable.

'Why, if you intend to stay on Amanos, can't you stay married to me?'

I didn't reply, and Matteo's eyes narrowed.

'Have you met someone else? Are you having an affair?'

'That's rich, coming from you.'

Matteo's affairs were plastered all over the tabloids, which was the whole reason I was meant to be invisible.

'*Are* you, Daisy?'

He looked furious, which was entirely unfair.

'As it happens, no, I am not.'

Something in my tone must have given me away because understanding flashed in his eyes like lightning.

'But you wish to?'

'No, actually. I have no desire to have seedy, sordid affairs the way you do,' I retorted.

'What, then?'

I shook my head, regretting having said anything about it. 'Let's focus on the annulment.'

'I need to know why.'

'No, you don't.'

'Yes, I do.'

I threw up my hands, exasperated. 'Matteo, you don't—'

'Not an affair...' he mused out loud. 'But something else. What could it be?'

Was he really so dense? Had the concept of true love really never occurred to him? Was it so off his radar that he couldn't imagine me or anyone else wanting it? Or was it that I was so unappealing to him he couldn't imagine anyone wanting me?

I shook my head, deciding to end his misery. 'I'm twenty-six years old, Matteo. I want a real marriage one day. A real family.'

I heard the ache of longing in my voice, and I knew he heard it too. A baby...that was what I really wanted. A family of my own—something I'd never had. I'd take the husband too, of course, but his image was a lot hazier.

'A family?' He looked surprised. 'You want children?'

'Yes—children, a husband, the lot. Most people do. Don't *you*?'

He was silent for a moment. 'I will need an heir eventually,' he said at last.

I spread my hands. 'There you go. We both need something other than a convenient marriage in name only. So this annulment works for both of us.'

'I already told you it doesn't for me.'

'Because of your grandfather?'

'Yes, because of him. As long as he is alive I must stay married—which you know.'

'You said it would no longer be an issue after two years.'

'Because I thought he would be *dead*.'

I flinched at that, because it sounded so horribly cold. Matteo swore under his breath and then whirled around on his heel, driving one hand through his ink-dark hair, making it ruffled in a way that would have been cute—except nothing about Matteo Dias was cute. He was dark, deadly, powerful, and incredibly charismatic. I felt drawn to him like a moth to dangerous flame, and unlike that hapless insect I *knew* I'd get burned.

Which was one of the reasons I wanted an annulment. Without Matteo Dias even on the periphery of my life there was far less danger of being singed. I'd already spent too much time poring over those magazine articles, wondering about the man I'd married and wishing he'd show a little interest in me. But I should have known someone as potently male, as powerful and autocratic as Matteo Dias, would balk at the idea of an annulment. He was a man who called the shots, who needed to be in control. And here I was, trying to take the reins.

Matteo turned around to face me, and that rush of incredulous rage had been replaced by something icily composed, leaving the angles of his beautiful face hard and unforgiving.

'I am not giving you an annulment.'

'You don't have any choice,' I shot back.

But inside I quailed. Matteo Dias had a lot more money and power than I did. Giving back his money was going to have me living on pennies, no matter what I'd told him. But I had to be free. I had to have a chance to pursue my dream of love and family—otherwise what point was there in anything?

But of course Matteo didn't understand that, and I had no desire to spell it out for him.

Looking at him now, I saw a new hardness in his eyes, felt the unrelenting iron in his soul, and

I wondered what had caused him to be so ruth-lessly unyielding. It reminded me that I knew nothing about this man beyond what I'd read in the tabloids and what he'd chosen to tell me when we'd first met.

I'd been at my lowest point then: six months in the city, out of cash and—in the last few sec-onds before we met—out of a job for slapping a man's hand away when he tried to grope me. But more than that, I'd been out of hope—and that was what had led me to consider Matteo's outrageous offer even for a second and then to accept it.

'I have a deal for you.'

Those were his first words to me. I was stand-ing on the street in the lashing rain, hugging my bag to my chest and waiting for the bus, when he came out of the diner from where I'd just been fired and walked straight towards me.

I glanced at him uncertainly, because he wasn't the sort of customer the rundown diner catered to. He was a dark beacon of privilege there on the grimy street, standing tall and proud and de-termined. I had no idea what he was doing there, much less what he wanted with me.

'A deal?' I eyed him warily, pretty sure that

any deal he offered would be one I'd want to refuse.

'Yes, a deal. I saw what happened back in the diner. You were fired for doing nothing but defending yourself. That was wrong.'

The quietly spoken statement, the certainty of it, reached me in a way nothing else had. Ever since I'd arrived in New York I'd been fending off people who wanted something for nothing, who were far too quick to swindle or lie or cheat. *Or attack...*

A simply spoken truth delivered by a stranger meant a lot...more than it should have.

'Thank you,' I managed, with as much as dignity as I could muster. 'Unfortunately it doesn't change anything.'

I had enough money for my bus fare and not much else, and I was already a month behind on my rent. I had no family, no friends, nowhere to go—and, worst of all, I wasn't sure I had the capacity to care about any of it any more.

'Actually, it could,' Matteo said quietly, his voice carrying a subtle, silky power. '*I* could. If you will but give me a few moments of your time.'

I eyed him suspiciously. I'd arrived in this city

full of wide-eyed optimism, ready and even eager to believe the best of everyone, but I'd wised up since then. At least I'd been trying to.

'I don't think so, mister.' I hunched my shoulder against the rain and peered down the street in the vain hope that a bus would lumber by soon.

Matteo gave a little reassuring smile. 'It's not that kind of deal, trust me.'

The way he said it made me flush, because *of course* it wasn't that kind of deal. He was way, way out of my league and we both knew it.

'This is perfectly respectable and legal—entirely above board.'

I eyed him warily. 'What, then?'

'I want you to marry me.'

I gaped. I couldn't process those six words; they bounced off my brain, refusing to make sense. Then, when the shock wore off, I looked around for the spectators, the punchline. Surely he was making fun of me?

Matteo must have seen something of that in my eyes, for he said quietly, 'No joke. I'm completely serious.'

He nodded towards a café a few doors down from the diner—a far nicer establishment than the one of my previous employment.

'Why don't we get out of the rain and talk through it for a few minutes?'

I hesitated, because my instinct was to say absolutely not. Only a few weeks ago I'd believed what a man had said and I'd paid for it—sorely. Surely I wasn't going to do it again? Especially when this man's so-called deal was obviously nonsensical?

'At least have a coffee on me,' he said.

And that was what sealed it. I was hungry and tired and wet, and I didn't even have the money for a cup of coffee.

'All right,' I said. 'One coffee.'

A few minutes later we were seated at a quiet table in the back of the café, and I had my hands around the comforting warmth of a large latte— an extravagance I hadn't had in for ever.

Matteo sat opposite me, sipping a double espresso, the shoulders of his suit coat damp from the rain. When I breathed in, I caught the cedar-scented aroma of his aftershave.

'So what *is* this deal, really?' I asked.

'What I said. I need to be married.' He gave me the flicker of a smile. '*Need* being the operative word. I'm not looking for a wife.'

I couldn't keep my mouth from curling up

in cynical bemusement. 'What *do* you require, then?'

'Just a legal document saying I'm married.' He took another sip of his espresso before resuming. 'I'll pay you a million euros up front and then two hundred and fifty thousand euros for every year we remain married. Your housing and all expenses will be provided, and we will never have to lay eyes on each other again.'

I shook my head slowly, unable to take it in. To take *him* in. Because he was so overwhelming, with his dark hair and steely eyes, his body made up of hard, powerful lines, each one emanating an authority I recognised even if I couldn't begin to imagine it.

One million euros.

It was crazy. *He* was crazy. And yet he didn't look crazy. He looked remarkably and alarmingly sane.

'Why do you need to get married so badly?' I asked in a shaky voice.

'Because my grandfather requires it before I take control of his company—which is something I very much wish to do.'

The words were terse, but I saw the way his jaw clenched and his hands briefly curled into fists, and I knew there was a great deal more to that complicated relationship than I could ever know or guess.

Still, I wondered, *why me?*

'Surely you have someone more suitable to ask.'

'I don't want someone "suitable".'

He smiled at me rather grimly before draining his espresso.

'I want someone unremarkable who will be glad for what I give her, not ask any awkward questions, and most of all stay out of my life, as well as out of the public eye.'

'So you want a wife who doesn't act like a wife?'

His smile gleamed white as he nodded his approval. 'Exactly.'

'I'm sure there are plenty of women who would accept the money you're offering. You hardly needed to approach a stranger like me.'

I shook my head, still sensing a catch. Matteo was way out of my league. Why not ask some grasping socialite? Someone with status and privilege and beauty? Most people, I'd found, would do a lot for money.

Matteo leaned back in his chair, crossing one

long, powerful leg over the other as he eyed me in consideration.

'Possibly, but I'm in a rush, and I don't want any complications with someone who might not view my offer with the gratitude I'd prefer.' He gave me a quick, cool smile. 'I'd like to keep my marriage quiet. I don't want it to…*hamper*…any of my activities.'

It took a few seconds for his meaning to sink in. 'You mean you don't want it to affect your other relationships?'

'I wouldn't call them *relationships*,' he answered with a quick, hard smile. 'But, yes, you have grasped the essentials.'

In a flash I understood why he'd asked me— because I was clearly desperate and would be pathetically grateful for what he was offering. And I wouldn't mind if he slept around while I stayed silent in the shadows.

I felt too tired to be stung, because of course he was right. I *was* desperate, as well as pathetic enough to be considering his offer seriously for the first time since he'd broached it. At least Matteo, unlike other people I'd met since moving to the city, was honest about his intentions.

'So,' I began slowly, 'we get married and you go on your merry way? That's it?'

'Not quite. I need you to move to the island of Amanos, off the coast of Greece, where I have a villa. It's a very pleasant place, and my home is exceedingly comfortable. You would want for nothing.'

That was quite a big addendum to this deal of his, and yet I had no ties to this city, much as I'd tried to make some. No ties anywhere. Still, I was cautious—and definitely cynical. I'd learned to be.

'Why there?' I asked.

He gave me the glimmer of a smile, but there was a warning in his eyes. 'You are currently not meeting my second requirement.'

I raised my eyebrows. 'Do you actually expect me to accept an offer such as yours, and move to a foreign country at that, without asking a few questions?'

Not that I was actually thinking of accepting it. At least not very much.

'Very well, I will explain it in detail,' he replied, leaning forward. 'But in actuality it is really very simple.'

His silvery gaze pinned me to where I sat.

'This will be a convenient marriage in name only—nothing more than a document to sign. No expectation of any relationship—physical, emotional, or otherwise. You will stay on Amanos so I know where you are, and can call on you if needed, but you will be out of the public eye. In a year—no more than two—the marriage will be annulled and you can go—how did you put it?— on your merry way, quite a bit richer.'

'Call on me "if needed"? What does that mean?'

He shrugged impatiently, barely more than a twitch of his powerful shoulders. 'I doubt it will be necessary.'

'But…?'

'In case my grandfather needs proof of some sort or wants to check on you…make sure I am indeed married. It is merely a precaution, that is all.'

And also a way for him to be in control, because I strongly suspected Matteo Dias was a man who needed to be in control of everything— including me. Something I resisted instinctively.

'And in a year or two?' I asked. 'Why would you annul the marriage then?'

'My grandfather has been diagnosed with cancer. He's not been given very long to live.'

He spoke so coldly that I drew back a little.

Matteo bared his teeth in a grim smile. 'As you are most likely able to surmise, we are not close.'

'So you want me to marry you and then live on some remote island for a maximum of two years?'

Not that it sounded so bad right then. I was a breath away from being homeless as it was. And yet it would be a prison of sorts, and it meant giving this man all the power—two things I really didn't like.

'There could be worse things, surely?'

Of course there could. And yet...

'Why should I trust you? I could agree and you could bundle me into the back of a van in the next second.'

Matteo's eyes flashed with ire, as if he disliked being accused in such a way. 'I could bundle you into the back of a van regardless of whether you agree or not. If you need some guarantees I shall put them in place.'

'How?'

He shrugged. 'Everything will be written in a legal contract and witnessed.'

I shook my head. 'That's not worth very much.

How do I know I can trust you not to take advantage?'

His gaze raked me from head to toe. 'Trust me, I will *not* take advantage.'

Ouch. My cheeks flushed and I focused my humiliated gaze on my coffee. Why was I even having this conversation?

'But if it makes you feel better, everything can be done in public—the contract, the marriage itself, your transport. I'll book a first-class ticket on a commercial airline.'

I hesitated, because it all sounded too good to be true, and I knew what *that* looked like. I knew what it *felt* like. Just the memory of Chris Dawson's leering face and grasping hands was enough to turn my stomach and make me want to hang my head in shame. Surely I'd wised up since then? Realised that people spouted honeyed words and then watched you get stuck in them?

'There must be some catch,' I protested.

'No catch.'

'There's *always* a catch.'

'This time there isn't.'

He placed one hand on my arm, making me jolt. A warm rush of longing swept through me, surprising me in its strength, because his touch was so clearly one of empathy rather than desire. I was smart enough to realise that this man did not think of me that way, and most likely never would—which was a good thing. That was a complication, not to mention a danger, I most certainly didn't need.

He gave me a smiling look of understanding and compassion, and its warmth strengthened that surge of longing in a way that made me feel deeply uneasy. It was one thing to be physically attracted to a man like Matteo Dias. That was inevitable. It was another matter entirely to connect with him emotionally—even for a second. Far, far too dangerous.

I pulled away and he dropped his hand.

'I understand why you'd be concerned. You've had a bad experience recently, and it's all too easy to be taken advantage of these days—especially when you are a young woman on your own. You *are* on your own?'

It was barely a question, and it grated that it was so obvious I had no one in my life—no boyfriend, no family, no friends, even. 'Yes.' I forced myself to give him a direct look. 'How did you know?'

Matteo shrugged. 'There is a…a loneliness about you. Like a mist.'

I looked away, hating the fact that my eyes were stinging at his surprisingly compassionate and yet brutally honest assessment. A loneliness like a mist? Yes, I felt that—cloaking me in its sadness even though I didn't want to be sad. I'd always tried to see the sunny side of life, to be optimistic even when there was little reason to be so. Sometimes it felt like the only good thing I had, but too many experiences lately had robbed me of my hope. My joy. And now this…

'So please,' Matteo continued, 'let me reassure you that this offer is entirely above board. I will draw up an agreement that will protect your rights as well as my own. If you come to the courthouse in an hour you can read and sign that agreement, and then I'll deposit the money in your bank account and arrange your travel to Athens. I can have someone meet you there, or you can arrange your own travel, if that makes you feel safer. Let someone know where you are going if you need a safeguard. Whatever you want. You'll be in control of everything, with zero risk.'

His mouth curved, his teeth flashing white as he read the name badge on my waitress uniform.

'Trust me, Daisy, this is your lucky day.'

And so it was—although I felt more anxious than excited when I met him at the courthouse an hour later.

We went over the contract in painstaking detail, although the numbers and words all blurred in my mind.

'Are you sure about this?' Matteo asked me seriously.

Again that surprising compassion warmed his eyes, making me do the one thing I'd been sure, right up until that moment, I wouldn't. I said yes.

Triumph blazed in his eyes then, and I wondered if I was crazy. Was I throwing my life away? My freedom and even my safety? I didn't know this man.

And yet something about him, despite his hard ruthlessness and innate arrogance, made me trust him. Stupidly, because I'd already learned not to trust people, and yet some stubborn part of me still kept wanting to.

Besides, I told myself, as Matteo had said, *I* would be in control. I watched him wire the money to my bank account. I saw him book the first-class ticket to Athens. He did both just minutes after the marriage ceremony, which was so fast I could have blinked and missed it. We exchanged no rings. We didn't even touch. It felt completely soulless, and yet it was legally binding.

Afterwards Matteo took my hands in his own, which were warm and dry and strangely comforting. He stared into my eyes, a smile curving his mouth, making him seem softer somehow. Kinder.

'Thank you, Daisy,' he said, and his voice was full of warmth.

Foolish me, my heart fluttered.

Foolish because the next words out of his mouth were, 'Hopefully we'll never have to see each other again.'

CHAPTER THREE

'I STILL DON'T understand why you want an annulment.'

Daisy Campbell—no, Daisy Dias—had surprised me a few too many times this evening, and this surprise was the most unwelcome one of all. I'd given her everything she could possibly want. Why would she want to hand it all back? It was the last thing I expected. The last thing I wanted.

I married Daisy Campbell both to satisfy and to spite my grandfather, and it was so very sweet to experience both when I tossed the marriage certificate on Bastian Arides's desk and informed him of my new status.

'You made a condition and it has now been met.'

'And your wife?' he asked, looking stunned by my bloodless coup.

I laughed as I told him the truth. 'A dumpy nobody of a waitress I picked up from a diner in

New York. She's currently residing on Amanos, in case you feel the need to check.'

Bastian's mouth dropped open; he'd expected me to marry some suitable socialite he could add to the family pedigree—some way, perhaps, to justify my place in his life, bastard grandson that I was. Little did he know me. Little did he realise how deep my need for vengeance, for justice ran.

'I think you'll find I've won, old man,' I said as I strolled out of his office. 'The condition you made to the board has been met in full.'

Bastian shook his head, his expression one of both defeat and fury. 'That is not what I meant, Matteo, and you know it.'

'Too bad you weren't more specific, then.'

The clause in the agreement to transfer his shares to me had been clear—marry, and stay married, in order to get his shares and sixty percent of the stock in Arides Enterprises, and therefore complete control of the company. The board had agreed; everyone had signed. And I'd done what he asked.

I had what I wanted and there was absolutely nothing he could do about it. I was now in control of Arides Enterprises—the company his father had built from scratch, the company he'd wanted to hand on to his *legitimate* grandson, Andreas.

But of course that was impossible. Instead he'd had to hand it to me, his only heir and the only person in the company capable of running a multimillion-dollar enterprise. The person who had taken the lagging sales and outdated practices and dragged them into the twenty-first century—and into the black.

Now, as I looked at my so-called dumpy waitress of a wife, I realised she was neither. She sparkled—and it wasn't just the dress. Her eyes glittered like topaz, her cheeks were flushed and her chest heaved. Everything about her seemed alive and shockingly vibrant. *Desirable.* How extraordinary. How unexpected. It made me pause, my mind reviewing everything she'd said.

'I told you—I want a chance at a real marriage,' she insisted. 'A family.'

'A family? The biological clock is ticking, I suppose?'

She folded her arms, her expression turning mutinous. 'Something like that.'

I could give her a baby.

It was a novel thought, and admittedly not entirely unwelcome. Yes, I needed an heir...eventually. It was something I'd postponed, put off to the misty, distant future because it hadn't felt urgent or necessary. And yet… I was thirty-six. The lifestyle I'd been living was starting to lose its appeal—at least a little. And I was already married.

Why would I want to bother with the hassle of courting some other woman when I had one right here? One I was, much to my own surprise, finding desirable?

Still, this would take some thought. Some planning. The last thing I wanted to do was rush into a lifetime commitment with someone who was still essentially a stranger.

And yet… Daisy was biddable. Acceptable. And she'd already agreed to a marriage of convenience. Why not a marriage that was convenient on slightly different terms?

'You're still young,' I remarked. 'Another year wouldn't make much difference to your plans.' Although for some reason the prospect my words implied irritated me.

'And is that how long it would be?' she countered. 'A few months ago I read in the paper that your grandfather is celebrating his unexpected all-clear from cancer.' Her lips twisted. 'Something I doubt you expected.'

Damn those nosy tabloids. 'I'm pleased he's had such successful treatment, of course,' I answered levelly.

He'd been declared in remission, rather than in the clear, but I wasn't going to debate the point. The truth was he'd lasted longer than anyone had expected—myself most of all.

'And you need to remain married for as long as he's alive, as I recall?'

Her golden-brown eyes met mine in challenge and held me there.

'Did you ever plan to inform me that the duration of our marriage was going to be a bit longer than you had said?'

'I assumed you were satisfied with the arrangement,' I stated coolly.

'You assumed wrong.'

Her voice was as cool as my own. When had she developed such confidence? Such poise? The woman I remembered from the diner had been beaten down by life, as well as frightened of its possibilities. I'd chosen her for exactly those reasons. And while, judging by her dress, Daisy might still need to develop some sense of style, she had plenty of courage.

I felt a flicker of admiration for her, and promptly suppressed it.

'Why not wait another year?' I pressed. 'I doubt it will be longer than that. Then you won't have to give back the money. You're giving up a lot, Daisy, and for what? A chance at something that might not even happen?'

Hurt flashed in her eyes as her chin went up. 'Thanks a lot.'

'There's no one at the moment, is there?' I reminded her, thinking that she had better not be lying to me about that. 'And you said you intend to stay on Amanos. Do you really think you're going to find Mr Right there?'

'I have better chance of doing so if I'm not married to Mr Wrong,' she retorted. 'Although perhaps I'll just *act* as if the marriage has been annulled if you refuse to agree it.'

Fury surged through me along with something else—something hot and molten and *fierce*. Although I suspected her words were nothing but an empty threat, they still had the power to enrage me.

'You will *not* go down that forsaken route,' I ground out. 'Is that clear?'

She shrugged, the movement of her slender shoulders tautening the material across her breasts.

'There's nothing about it in our agreement. I don't have to be faithful, since you certainly haven't been. I could even have a child without you.' Her eyes flashed fire. 'Consider this nothing more than a courtesy call.'

My fists clenched. 'I will *not* be made a cuckold so you can have an illegitimate child.' I spoke savagely, memories pounding through me in a relentless tide of rejection.

You're nothing but a bastard. You were born one, you will remain one, and you will die one.

I certainly wouldn't countenance another one being brought into the world, for that was what it would be if Daisy had a child that was not my own.

'I hardly think that's what we're talking about here.'

Daisy's chin was still lifted, but her lips trembled. She wasn't as confident as she pretended. The thought brought satisfaction, as well as a surprising shaft of disappointment. Some contrary part of me had enjoyed her boldness.

'And you can't exactly call yourself cuckolded considering we've never…?' Her voice wavered and she looked away.

'We've never…?' I prompted silkily.

My blood was flowing hotly through my veins and that slinky tube of a dress was begging to be peeled off her curvaceous body. What I'd insisted I would never do suddenly seemed like a very good idea. The *right* idea, all things considered. I could prove a point, and do it quite pleasurably.

'You know what I mean,' Daisy said, her voice little more than a whisper.

'What I know,' I replied as I closed the distance between us so that I could feel the heat rolling off her body and she could feel it off mine, 'is that a few minutes ago you told me you wanted a baby.'

Her lips parted and her eyes widened in realisation. 'Not *yours.*'

'And yet I'm your husband,' I remarked. 'Wanting my baby is the most sensible idea, really.'

'N…no,' she stammered. 'It isn't.'

Her skin was pale golden and freckled and

she smelled of vanilla and almonds. *Delicious.*
I lifted my hand and traced the pure line of her
collarbone with the tip of my finger.

She shuddered under my touch and took a step
back. 'You're taking this all wrong.'

'I really don't think I am.'

'What happened to marriage in name only?'

Yes, what *had* happened to it? It was starting
not to seem like such a good idea. Distantly I
remembered the original purposes for my marriage—to spite my grandfather and keep living
my life the way I wanted to. And yet somewhere,
tangled up in all that, had been the desire to do
some good to someone and even be honourable
about it—although whether I'd achieved those
aims was debatable.

Yet all of it—all my resolutions and all my re-
venge—went up in smoke as I looked at Daisy
standing in front of me, a flame of beauty, firing my own desire. In this moment all I wanted
was her.

'Perhaps,' I said, 'we should renegotiate the
terms of our arrangement.'

Matteo's eyes turned the colour of smoke as he
took another deliberate step towards me, his in-

tent clear in every taut line of his body. I remained rooted to the spot, unable to move, to *think*. I'd never expected this—the heat in his eyes, the sure touch of his hand. The mere caress of his fingertips on my collarbone had sent arrows of exquisite sensation shafting through me. If he touched me again...

Why did that feel like a promise?

'Matteo, you've made it very clear that you want a marriage in name only.'

My voice and legs both shook as I managed a step backwards, away from this sudden new temptation. I'd always known Matteo was handsome, appealing, *sexual*. But I'd thought I was strong enough, *smart* enough, to stay immune. Clearly I wasn't.

'Don't mess that up just because your pride is dented by my asking for an annulment,' I said, trying to sound reasonable instead of terrified... and tempted. So, so tempted.

'This isn't about pride, Daisy. It's about desire.'

His voice was as smooth as silk, so assured as it flowed over me. He took a step closer, close enough that I could breathe the woodsy scent of him again, and it made me dizzy.

'I meant—' I began, my voice wobbling, but

I was silenced by the touch of his hands spanning my waist.

'And this is what *I* meant.'

His palms were warm and strong through the thin material of my dress, pulling me towards him. I gasped out loud as he captured my mouth in a kiss that demanded—and I gave.

I'd been kissed only once before in my life, by a man I'd found odious. As Matteo's lips came down on mine I instinctively braced myself for a similar experience—bad breath, slimy tongue, pawing hands.

It took only a millisecond for me to realise how ridiculous that notion was, how little I had to fear, and yet at the same time how much. Matteo's kiss was as different from the first one I'd had as the ocean to a mud puddle.

His mouth *possessed* mine as he explored it with sensual thoroughness, obliterating thought and weakening my knees, his tongue and lips moving in a dance as old as the ages and yet feeling startlingly new. How could a kiss do so much? It was practically a weapon.

But he didn't stop with a kiss. His hands moved from my waist to my breast, his palm cupping it with that same deft and shocking assuredness, his thumb running over the peak. I mewled. I actually *mewled*. I felt as if I didn't know myself any more—this creature who melted like candle wax, who clamoured for more. Because I wanted more from him—more than a kiss, a caress. In that moment I wanted it all.

Without even realising what I was doing, I clenched my hands on the lapels of his tuxedo and opened my mouth under his, inviting him in. I stood on my tiptoes and swayed as he anchored his hands on my hips and tugged me towards him.

My hips collided with that particularly impressive and overwhelming part of his anatomy, and it was enough to send a blast of icy realisation through me.

I stumbled back.

What was I doing? What was *he* doing?

'Don't!' I managed to gasp, even though everything in me was reeling, my senses exploding like fireworks as if my whole body had come alive under his hands, my skin still prickling with need.

'Are you sure you mean that?'

Besides a slight flush on his blade-like cheekbones, Matteo looked remarkably unaffected. He sank his hands into his pockets, his gaze terribly cool. The realisation that his kiss had affected me far more than it had him was utterly humiliating, and sudden unfortunate tears stung my eyes.

'Yes, I do.'

'I think I could convince you otherwise.'

Already the flush had left his face and he stood there, the archetype of assured arrogance, his shoulders thrust back, his jaw set, his eyes glittering—while I was still raggedly panting, my heart rate skittering all over the place.

'Only to prove a point,' I choked out as I willed my flush to fade and my heart to slow. 'You've told me enough times already.'

'What?'

He raised his eyebrows, sounding distinctly nonplussed by my statement. Did he not remember? Had he not realised how insultingly clear he'd been about making sure this was a marriage in name only? Didn't he recall the scathing look he'd given me, the reassurance that he would have no need to take advantage?

Which, of course, had been what I wanted too. *Still* wanted. It was just that his contrary kiss had rocked me for a second. I was already recovering—or so I told myself.

I lifted my chin, heedless of the tears that I knew still sparkled in my eyes. 'Come on, Matteo. You've made it very clear that you don't find me…desirable.' Stupidly, it hurt to say the words out loud.

Matteo gave me a smugly amused look, his lips curving, a surprising dimple appearing in one cheek. I realised I'd never actually seen him smile before—not properly.

'I think I just proved to you otherwise.'

'You were proving something,' I agreed, unable to keep hurt from lacing every word. 'But I think it had more to do with power than need.'

The dark slashes of his eyebrows drew together in a frown. 'What is that supposed to mean?'

'You didn't want me going ahead with an annulment…doing something that isn't sanctioned and signed off by you. I get it.'

I shook my head, suddenly exhausted, both emotionally and physically, with the aftershocks of his touch still zinging through me. It had taken all my emotional reserves to survive this encounter, after three years of peace and quiet and solitude.

What had I been *thinking*, coming here with my request? Knowing Matteo Dias would refuse it? Because I realised that while I still longed for a child, a family, the need as deep and fervent as ever, I didn't have the strength to fight my husband for my freedom. Not when he held all the cards and had all the power.

'You think that's why I kissed you?' Matteo demanded, sounding irritated by the idea.

I raised my shoulders in a weary shrug. 'Are you saying differently—that you were suddenly overcome by passion for me and couldn't control yourself?' I let out a humourless laugh. 'As if.'

Matteo's frown deepened and he didn't reply. His narrowed gaze was assessing and, I feared, would dismiss me in the space of a few seconds.

'No, of course not,' he said finally. 'Don't be absurd.'

His words should have vindicated me, but they only deflated me further. Of *course* that hadn't been the case. He'd just been using me to prove a point—and suddenly I couldn't bear it. I thought of the loathsome Chris Dawson again, the look of revulsion on his face as I stumbled away.

Do you honestly think you're worth that much, sweetheart? You're deluded.

I thought I'd wised up since then, but I could see now that I was still under the most unbearable delusion—thinking that someone like Matteo Dias would agree to my plan and bend to my will, even desire me as a woman, rather than make me a point to be proved.

In that moment I couldn't fathom why I had come here at all. Had it simply been a perfect storm of memory and loss? The anniversary of my parents' death, the marriage of my closest friend back on Amanos, the feeling that, as happy and busy as I was, I was still alone?

I was always alone, and I would always be alone as long as I was married to this man.

'Never mind, Matteo.' I choked the words out, wanting only to escape his ruthless, arrogant sneer and get to the solitude and safety of my hotel room. 'I've changed my mind. I'll stay married to you. For another year, at least.'

I whirled around far too fast in my slinky dress and towering heels. I started to stumble and I gasped, flinging my hands out to break my inevitable fall, but then Matteo steadied me, his hands warm and firm on my shoulders.

'Daisy…' he said in a low voice.

He sounded…what? Sad? Apologetic? Or just exasperated at the fact that he'd had to deal with me at all and that I wasn't doing as he bade?

'I'll leave for Amanos in the morning,' I said, and, wrenching myself out of his arms, I hurried blindly from the room.

CHAPTER FOUR

WHAT HAD JUST HAPPENED?

Daisy had left—that was what. And I had kissed her. A shockingly pleasurable kiss that had left me aching in a way I hadn't in a long time. In fact, in living memory.

I released a shuddering breath as I raked a hand through my hair, my heart thudding a little too hard for my liking. And yet I also felt invigorated, fully alive, as if that kiss had shocked something dormant inside me and sprung it into life.

I was pulsing with both memory and desire even as I was trying to make sense of Daisy's words, her hurt. She thought I didn't desire her, when surely even the most innocent woman would have realised that I obviously did. And yet I had been as surprised by my desire as Daisy had—if not more so. I'd never expected to *want* the woman, and certainly not in the way that I had—with explosive and alarming force, as if a tsunami had crashed over the both of us, pulling us under.

I might have started to kiss her to prove a point, but it had become something else entirely. Something outrageous and overwhelming—even now I was half tempted to chase after her and prove to her just how much I desired her and how much she desired me. I'd felt it in the way her mouth had opened under mine, her hands pulling at my shoulders, drawing me to her.

The memory alone was enough to send heat searing through my body, and I took a step forward before I stilled.

No. I did not chase after women. And certainly not the likes of Daisy, wife or not. I should be relieved that she clearly regretted her ridiculous impulse to ask for an annulment. She'd leave for Amanos in the morning, and if I had my preference I'd never see her again—which was how I'd always wanted it.

So why did the prospect unsettle me? It almost made me feel guilty—as if I'd treated Daisy badly, when I knew I had not. I had given her a fortune, a home to live in, and required nothing from her save that she stay put. If she was no longer satisfied with the arrangement we'd agreed on, that was her fault—not mine.

And yet… I couldn't get the image of her out of my mind. The ridiculous red dress that had highlighted her figure in such a breathtaking display, her cloud of light brown hair and the fractured hurt in her topaz eyes. And the reality was pressing in on me that I would need an heir. A proper wife. And the one I currently had might actually fit the bill. After all, Daisy had been happy enough with our convenient marriage. Why shouldn't she be satisfied with what I had to offer her now—the ability to have a child, a family of her own? She could even stay on Amanos, as was her preference. And my own life wouldn't have to change—at least not much.

Could it be that simple? Was it what I really wanted?

Mulling it over, I headed back to the party.

'Matteo, you've been gone for ages.'

A skinny arm wound through my own as my companion for the evening pouted prettily up at me, no doubt thinking she looked seductive rather than petulant. I stared down at her, trying to remember her name.

'Matteo?'

'I had some business to take care of.'

I reached for a glass of champagne from a nearby waiter's tray and drained it in one long swallow. Daisy's image was still flashing behind my eyes. Those hurt eyes. Why did they unsettle me so much? I'd managed to completely forget Daisy for three years. Why couldn't I get her out of my mind now?

'Business?'

The woman whose name I couldn't remember deepened her pout, making her look like a sulky child. Did she honestly think that was alluring, or that I would care? I gazed down at her expertly made-up face and registered the calculation in her eyes.

As if on cue, she nestled closer to me.

'This party's rather dull, isn't it? How about we go upstairs?'

She gave me a knowingly seductive look that normally would have had me smiling just as knowingly back, but for some reason it made my stomach clench and my body recoil. I didn't want this woman. I wanted another one—with topaz eyes and a ridiculous red dress.

'Matteo…?'

On any other evening I would have taken up

this woman's offer—and gladly. I'd arranged my marriage to satisfy my grandfather's vindictive demand and also to grant me the minimum of inconvenience—and for the last three years I had been inconvenienced very little indeed. Yet now I thought of the paltry pleasures available to me and realised how little they appealed.

It was a strange thought, but I realised it was not a new one. Those pleasures had been palling for some time, and it had simply taken one shocking encounter with my wayward wife to make me realise it.

'I'm busy tonight,' I told the woman—Veronique, I'd remembered—and watched, unmoved, as her mouth dropped open in surprise and then her eyes narrowed.

'It's not that frumpy tramp, is it?' she asked.

A sudden red-hot rage blazed through me. 'You will not talk about her like that,' I snapped.

Veronique's expression managed to turn both smug and desolate. 'It *is* her, then?'

I turned away without replying. Yes, it was her—frustratingly so—but I was not about to explain anything to the woman I'd just dismissed and forgotten. I strode through the ballroom, intent on assuaging this sudden, unsettling restlessness that surged through me.

I had any number of ways to do so, I told myself as I surveyed the ballroom, with its bevy of beautiful women, nearly any of whom would be happy to accompany me just about anywhere. A few caught my eye and smiled hopefully, but I looked away from them all, uninterested.

And that was the heart of the problem, I realised. I was restless in a way I hadn't been before, and the pleasures that I had always enjoyed now seemed pointless and empty. It was as if I'd plumbed my soul and found unexpected depths. I wanted more than a one-night stand or a meaningless affair—more than yet another round of parties and social occasions to fill my evenings.

This had been building for a while, but now the ache was impossible to ignore. I was thirty-six years old and I felt jaded by life's pleasures, too weary to want them any longer. But did I really want a *wife*? A *real* one?

'You're looking rather lonely, Matteo.'

I turned to see Lara, a woman I knew only as an acquaintance, sidling up to me. I smiled thinly at her and she cocked her head.

'Perhaps you want company?'

She was beautiful, with long, tumbling black hair and vivid blue eyes, her mouth pursed in a provocative pout, her generous figure encased in ice-blue silk. An international lawyer, I remembered, based in London.

Already I could imagine how the evening would unfold—a bit of flirting, a few nuanced innuendoes, the building of expectation and then upstairs to bed. It had been a pleasurable dance for so long, but now it just felt like so many tired steps.

She'd leave sometime in the night—or I would; I never slept a whole night with a woman. Perhaps we'd see each other again...perhaps not. Rinse and repeat. And yet right now it felt like the last thing I wanted. It felt like a burden rather than a pleasure, and one I had absolutely no interest in.

Did this happen to everyone at one time or another? Or had Daisy done something to me with her fiery determination, her sudden hurt—and that kiss?

Oh, that kiss.

'Matteo?' Lara's speculative gaze rested on my face, uncertain and a bit impatient.

Even as I contemplated taking her up on her

offer, if only just to banish this strange new sickness that seemed to have taken me over, I shook my head. 'I have work to do,' I said, and turned on my heel.

I strode out of the ballroom, uncaring of the whispers that followed in my wake. No doubt most people had seen Daisy confront me a short while ago, and now they saw me leaving in a hurry. The rumours would spark and fly—something I had always been keen to avoid—but now...

Now I really didn't care.

I headed to the hotel bar and ordered a whisky, neat, throwing it back with grim intention. I was on the brink of making a big decision and I needed to be sure. Did I want Daisy that much? Was I willing to bind her to me for ever? And what about the needed heir? A child? Was I ready to take on that responsibility?

Briefly I pictured myself locked away, being told I was worthless, tormented simply because of my parentage. Anger still burned at the rank injustice and cruelty of it—the injustice and cruelty I'd been subjected to again and again, not just by my grandfather but by his savage minion, Eleni.

My lips twisted at the name.

Would having my own child heal that old wound in some small way? Was I capable of being a good father in a way my own father and grandfather had not been?

Did I even want to try?

I laid my hands flat on the bar, ideas and implications racing through me. Was I willing to give up my way of life for something else? Something perhaps better?

An image floated through my mind—a little boy with grey eyes, a young girl with light brown hair. A sudden shaft of longing pierced me unexpectedly, and I nearly gasped from the strength of it.

Could I possibly be thinking this way? Wanting a child when I'd always said I did not? Wanting a life I'd never actually envisaged for myself? And what about Daisy?

I could handle her, I decided. She would bend to my will as she had before. This marriage might no longer be quite as convenient, but it would still be on my terms.

'Wake up, Daisy.'

Sleep blurred my brain and clouded my vision as I slowly blinked the world into focus. The first thing I saw was the clock by the side of the bed in my hotel room—half past seven in the morning. The second thing I saw was Matteo Dias, standing at the end of my bed.

'*What?*'

The word came out in a high-pitched screech as I scooted upright, clutching the duvet to me in maidenly modesty. I was wearing a roomy T-shirt and shorts as pyjamas, but still...

'What on earth are you doing here?'

'I want to talk to you.'

Matteo seemed unconcerned that he'd invaded my hotel room at a decidedly early hour. He looked remarkably well put together, considering the time, dressed in a grey pinstriped suit with a starched blue shirt and cobalt tie, his hard jaw freshly shaven, his dark hair still slightly damp from a shower. He looked wonderful, and I hated that fact.

'How did you get into my hotel room?' I demanded, my senses still spinning simply from having him here.

'I asked the concierge to let me in.'

'What?' I could scarcely believe it. 'And he did? That's a total invasion of my privacy!'

'You're my wife,' Matteo replied with a shrug,

seemingly unconcerned by the gross misconduct of the hotel staff.

'When it suits you,' I snapped.

I was at a distinct disadvantage, sitting in bed with what I suspected was a terrible case of bed-head and a pair of short pyjamas, while he was looking as if he'd just stepped out of a business meeting.

'I'm going to make an official complaint to the hotel.'

'Then you can do so to me. I own it.'

I gawped at him for a few seconds. 'Oh,' I said finally, feebly.

I knew Matteo was CEO of a real estate company, of course, but I had never known how vast or wealthy it—and he—was, although I expected *very* was the answer to both. I certainly hadn't realised he owned the place when I'd booked myself in.

'Even so…' I managed to rally. 'You shouldn't abuse your privilege like that.'

Another shrug was all the apology I got.

'I wished to speak with you before you left for Amanos and this was the most expedient way of doing so.'

'Why?' I asked irritably. I scooted out of bed

and snatched the thick terry cloth dressing gown off the bathroom door, swathing myself in it for protection. I still had bedhead, but at least I wasn't half naked. 'I hardly think there is anything left to discuss.'

'Actually, there is. I've ordered breakfast. Why don't we discuss it while we eat?'

'That sounds remarkably civilised,' I harrumphed.

In fact, I *was* hungry. I'd missed dinner last night, intent on finding Matteo. With little choice, anyway, I followed him into the suite's small sitting room. I'd dithered about staying in such a top-drawer hotel, but I'd wanted to be near to the ball and I'd justified the expense by asking for the hotel's cheapest room—which was still luxurious by my standards.

Now I wondered what the concierge must have thought this morning, discovering that the owner's wife had requested such a thing.

'Here we are.'

All urbane hospitality, Matteo began taking the domed lids off several silver dishes, and the tantalising aroma of freshly baked croissants wafted out.

'Coffee?' he asked, so very solicitously, as I sat down.

'Yes, please.'

I watched as he loaded up a plate with croissants and fresh fruit, wondering what on earth he was doing here. What could he possibly want from me?

My stomach cramped at the possibilities—as well as at the scorching memory of that kiss last night. A punishing, *proving* kind of kiss, and it made me cringe in shame at how I'd responded to it.

Matteo handed me the plate of food and a cup of steaming coffee before sitting down opposite me.

'Now,' he said with a smile. 'We can talk.'

He was being friendlier than I'd ever seen him before—although admittedly that was a total of two times.

After leaving Matteo last night I'd escaped to my room, longing to forget my own folly. As smart as I liked to think I'd become over the last few years, there was still a bit too much of the country bumpkin's wide-eyed optimism about me. I'd convinced myself I was being savvy and proactive, going to find my husband and ask for an annulment, but I realised last night I'd just been horribly naïve.

Of course Matteo wasn't going to give me what I wanted, and of course I wouldn't be able to get it without his consent. Worse, I'd started to wonder why it even mattered. Matteo was right; Mr Right wasn't waiting for me in Amanos or anywhere. Why bother upending my life on the off-chance I'd find a man who most likely didn't exist?

'What do you want to talk about?' I asked now—because surely it was better to know than not?

Matteo sat back in his chair, sipping his coffee. 'I've changed my mind,' he said, his voice as unruffled as if he were talking about a slight alteration to his plans for the day. 'I wish to re-negotiate the terms of our marriage.'

I eyed him warily, suspicious of his rather smug look—much like the typical cat with the cream, except Matteo was more of a tiger. Last night, curled up in bed, I'd heartily wished I'd never come to Athens to track him down, and even almost wished that I'd never married him in the first place.

Although, despite everything, I couldn't quite make myself wish that…

'Well?' he said, dark eyebrows arched. 'Aren't you curious?'

'Nervous, more like. Suspicious.'

'Suspicious! I've always treated you fairly, Daisy.'

I could hardly argue with that. A million euros was hardly unfair. And yet at the same time, I knew Matteo had had all the power, all the time, and that seemed unfair. I was at his mercy, whether I wanted to be or not…and I was afraid we both knew it. He certainly did.

'Why don't you just tell me what you want?' I said, trying to sound briskly practical and most likely failing. 'Then we'll go from there.' *Or not.*

'Very well.'

Matteo put down his coffee cup and leaned forward, his look of intent both purposeful and predatory. I tried not to shrink back. Tried not to remember how persuasive his kiss had been, his *hands*… No, I most certainly did not want to think about that right now.

'I've decided I wish to make our marriage… real.'

'Real…?' I repeated dumbly. Surely he couldn't

mean what my mind had foolishly leapt to because of that awful, amazing kiss? 'Our marriage *is* pretty real, Matteo. Signed and everything.' I laughed weakly.

'No, *glykia mou*, it is not. Most definitely not. But it will be.'

His teeth gleamed as he smiled and I simply stared. 'What does *glykia mou* mean?' I asked after a moment, because I couldn't process anything else about his statement just yet. After three years on Amanos, I could speak some Greek but that phrase escaped me.

Matteo's smile widened. 'My sweet.'

As if I was anything of the sort. I shook my head, putting my plate and cup down, my appetite vanished. If he meant what I thought he meant, there was no way I could agree. No way I could let myself even consider it—because after that kiss, part of me was dangerously tempted.

'However "real" you want to make this marriage, Matteo, I'm not interested.'

'Are you sure about that?'

'Yes, very sure.' I stood up, clutching the dressing gown around me. 'I never should have come here. I was very happy with the way things were. *Are.*'

Matteo cocked his head, his gaze sweeping slowly and thoroughly over me. 'Were you really, Daisy? Because I don't think you would have gone to such lengths to find me if you were.'

I opened my mouth to say something but no words came. He was right, of course. The desire, the *need* for a husband and family of my own, was as strong as ever—but it was one I'd just have to live with. I'd lived with it this long already, and who knew? Maybe one day I would find that Mr Right Matteo had scoffed about, even if in my leaden heart I doubted he existed.

Even so, Matteo Dias was too dangerous for me to tangle with any more than I already had. He was especially dangerous when he wanted something, and I realised right then how lucky I'd been, how *safe*, when Matteo hadn't been thinking about me at all.

'You grew up with your grandmother, did you not?' he remarked suddenly, and my mouth opened again—this time in shock.

Speechless, I stared at him. 'How did you know that?' I finally managed.

'I did a bit of research last night.'

'Now who's stalking?'

He shrugged. 'It is always useful to be informed.'

For what reason? And why on earth had he changed his mind about all this? I was afraid to ask, to *know*.

'Yes, I grew up with my grandmother,' I told him shortly. 'My mother died in a car accident when I was a baby and my father was never around.'

'So you've never had any real family?'

His assessment was brutally to the point. 'My grandmother was my family,' I protested, although I wasn't sure why.

My granny had done her duty, but it had not been tempered with much love. She'd been tired, broke, worn out from working her fingers to the bone cleaning other people's houses. I could hardly blame her for not wanting to take on a baby at her age, or for not having enough room in her heart to love me the way I'd ached to be loved.

'But not much family,' Matteo said quietly, watching me. 'Not the kind of family you really want, I think, because that's what has motivated you to find me, isn't it? Not so much wanting Mr Right as being *Mrs* Right? The mother.'

I gaped at him, shocked at how he'd cut to the heart of it. Of *me*. How had he discovered so much, so quickly? And not just the bare facts of my upbringing, which I supposed were easy enough to dig up, but the desires of my heart that I'd spoken of to no one. It unsettled me and touched me in equal measure that he saw those. That he seemed to understand them. And I knew the latter reaction was far more dangerous than the former.

'So what are you suggesting?' I asked hoarsely.

I couldn't make myself say the words, but Matteo said them for me.

'We'll have a family together,' he said. 'A real family, and a real marriage.' His smile widened as he held my gaze. 'We'll both get what we want.'

Daisy stared at me, her face draining of colour, her body lost in that enormous robe. I waited, sure she'd see the sense in my plan. How could she not?

I'd spent most of the night considering it in all its detail, as well as considering any potential objections Daisy might have—all of which seemed negligible. She wanted a family, a baby, and she would get one. And I would get what *I* wanted…an heir and an end to this restless ache. My convenient wife made just a little bit *more* convenient.

'Well?' I asked when she simply stared at me, her face very pale. 'What do you think?'

'What do I *think*?' she repeated, the last word ending in a yelp. 'I think you're *crazy*, Matteo Dias. And I think I will respectfully and firmly decline your offer of a *real* marriage, thanks anyway.'

With that she whirled around and stalked back to the bedroom, slamming the door behind her.

That was unexpected. I sat there for a moment, sifting through her words in my mind, trying to discern what was really bothering her. Daisy wanted a baby, she'd already reconsidered the annulment, and she was most certainly attracted to me—something I would happily prove to her again, and with ease. What on earth could her objection be?

Fighting irritation at her theatrics, I stood up and strode to the door, annoyed to find it locked.

'Open up, Daisy. We're not finished with our discussion.'

'We most certainly are,' she snapped back, 'and, anyway, I'm getting dressed.'

I folded my arms, tapping my foot as I counted to one hundred for form's sake. 'You must be dressed by now.'

'You're right—I am.'

She flung the door open and I blinked at her. She was dressed in faded jeans and a loose top that somehow made her look even more appealing, the clothes merely hinting at her lovely figure rather than highlighting it. Why had I never noticed how delicious she was, her curves in perfect proportion to the rest of her? Or that she had pale golden freckles across her nose and shoulders, like a spattering of gold dust, that matched the topaz of her eyes? Eyes, I saw now, that were glittering with both hurt and fury.

'Why are you so angry?' I asked, keeping my voice deliberately mild. 'I thought you would be pleased.'

'Pleased!' She choked the word out. 'Only you, Matteo, could ever think such a thing. You are so seriously deluded it's almost funny—except, of course, it's not. It's not funny at *all*.'

She shouldered her way past me as I held on to my temper with effort. 'I assure you, I am not deluded. My plan makes complete and utter sense, and I expect you will see that once you put this unwarranted emotional reaction aside.'

'And you're doing a really good job of convincing me.' She shook her head in disbelief as she moved past me.

'Where are you going?' I demanded, for she had a bag over one shoulder and was now shoving her feet into sandals.

'Back to Amanos.'

Fury bit deeper. This was most vexing. I'd expected her to be surprised, perhaps a bit taken aback, but not so scathingly incredulous and, worse, dismissive. No one dismissed me. Not any more.

'Not until we've finished our discussion,' I barked, but she didn't even look at me as she responded.

'We've finished it. I'm not making this marriage any more real than it already is.'

She turned to me, her expression fierce, and everything about her was vibrant and glittering.

'And if you want to annul the marriage instead, that will be fine by me. Go ahead. Make my day. Like I said, I'll give you the money back—every last euro.'

I stared at her, unimpressed by her display of histrionics, although I suspected in that moment she meant it. Clearly she needed to see sense. 'I have to say you're reacting very emotionally to what is an eminently sensible idea.'

Daisy threw her head back and laughed once— a wild, ragged sound that slipped under my sensibilities and touched me somehow.

'Exactly,' she said. 'You've hit the nail on the head right there.'

It took me a few crucial seconds to decipher her meaning. 'You dislike how sensible I'm being about marriage?'

'About a *real* marriage.'

She dropped her bag to level me with a look that felt bleak and powerful in its honesty, like a fist to the gut. I did my best to remain unmoved.

'I can just about live with myself, Matteo, for marrying you for convenience and money, even though it felt wrong. I was at such a low point when you asked me, with no friends, no money, nowhere to go and, worse, no hope. You were like a knight, riding in on your white charger, rescuing me. But you're *not* a knight, and I don't need to be rescued any more. I certainly don't need your version of a "real" marriage and family, whatever you think that looks like—because I assure you it is *not* the same as the way I see it.'

'How can you possibly know that?' I demanded. I disliked the way she was twisting events—as if I'd somehow exploited her, when we both knew she'd been given a very good deal.

'You've said enough to make me perfectly aware.'

'I've barely said anything,' I retorted, my temper rising and breaking through. 'You haven't *listened*.'

'I've heard enough.'

'Enough to presume you know what a real marriage between us would look like?' I countered. 'Why don't you enlighten me, then?'

She shook her head slowly. 'I don't think you even know what a real marriage *is*.'

That stung more than it should. 'And you do?'

'Not from personal experience, obviously, but I know that when and if I do marry—*really* marry—I'll do so for love.'

She made a face, as if she anticipated my reaction.

'I'm not pretending I know Mr Right is out there waiting for me, but I still hope one day after our marriage is annulled that I'll find him.

Because the truth is…' Her voice turned jagged and she took a deep breath to compose herself. 'The truth is,' she resumed, 'I want more than what you can offer me—and I'm not talking about some more stupid euros, or even the baby you've guessed I want so much. I want to love someone and be loved, Matteo.'

I must have grimaced without realising it, because she laughed and nodded.

'Yes, I'm quite sure that horrifies you. Don't worry—I get that. Your lifestyle has made that abundantly clear. But I'm different from you and I want to know what love feels like, because I never have, and I'm *quite* sure those concepts are not part of the scenario you're suggesting.'

I kept my expression composed, although her words had rocketed through me. *Love.* I'd assumed—erroneously, it seemed—that a woman who had agreed to a convenient marriage, who had lived it out for three years, accepting an outrageous sum of money as her due, would not be so deluded by the whole illusion and mockery of *love*. Clearly I would have to disabuse her of the notion.

'So you are refusing my proposal out of hand

simply because of a misguided belief you have in the idea of *love*,' I stated.

Daisy let out another one of those disconcertingly wild laughs. 'You've got it in one. Although it's not so much a proposal as a *proposition*, is it? Since I've already accepted your proposal.'

She shook her head, as if at her own folly, and I decided I'd had enough of her scorn, such as it was.

'I think you're mistaken, Daisy.'

'And I think *you* are, so we're at an impasse.'

'Are we?' I took a step towards her and watched as her pupils flared. An impasse, indeed. 'I really don't think we are.'

'Don't do that,' she warned me, her voice wobbling as colour surged into her lovely face.

I raised my eyebrows. 'Do what?'

'That...that *smoulder*. Seriously, I'm warning you.'

'Smoulder?' I pretended affront. 'You make me sound like some cartoon character.'

'You can't convince me, Matteo, no matter what you do.'

'Now, that,' I murmured, 'sounds like a challenge...'

Daisy stood stock-still, her bag at her feet, her

eyes wide, everything about her waiting. If she'd really been serious about what she'd said she would have left already. Instead she stood right in front of me, her body trembling like a flower in the wind, and didn't move at all.

'It wasn't meant to be a challenge,' she said, her voice little more than a breathless whisper.

I had her already and I hadn't even touched her. The knowledge was intoxicating. Electrifying. Because I wanted her as much as she wanted me. Desire pulsed between us like a live wire, connecting us, drawing us closer with a crackle.

'Matteo…' She licked her lips and shook her head, but still she didn't move.

'This feeling between us is unexpected, isn't it?' I murmured as I wrapped a tendril of her hair around my finger and pulled ever so gently. 'I think it's taken us both by surprise.'

'You don't…' she began feebly.

I tugged a little harder, drawing her towards me. 'I think you'll find that I do.'

Her hips bumped mine and she looked up at me unsteadily. 'Why are you doing this?'

'Because I want to. And because you want me to. Do you deny it?'

It felt important that she be honest with me, at least in this.

'No,' she whispered brokenly as her eyes fluttered closed.

And then I kissed her.

She tasted just as sweet as she had last night, her mouth opening under mine as her head fell back and I plundered her soft depths. And no matter how much I tasted, I felt only a deeper need for more.

Her body was soft and pliant under my hands, the dip of her waist fitting my palm so perfectly. I slid my hand under her loose top, felt her skin like silk beneath my questing fingers, the lovely fullness of her breast resting in my palm. She was perfect. Surprising, but perfect.

'Matteo…'

My name was a moan on her lips and I liked it that way. I liked it very much. I backed her against the door, pressing against her, thrilling to the way one slender leg slipped between mine and hooked around my calf. Now she was the one pulling me closer, and I went gladly. The only problem was the number of clothes we were both still wearing.

I unsnapped her jeans, my hand sliding towards the silky depths hidden there, and her whole body tensed.

'No, we can't...'

'We can, I assure you.'

I kissed her again, to remind her just how much we were both enjoying this, but with what felt like superhuman effort Daisy wrenched herself away.

'*No.* No, I won't be had like some—some harlot against a door!' Tears glittered in her eyes.

I tamped down on the sexual frustration roaring through me. 'I think we could have made it to the bed.'

'No, you don't get it at all.' She shook her head despairingly. 'And you never will. Because you—you don't even understand what a relationship is, Matteo. I've read the tabloids—'

So that was how she'd formed her opinion of me? I suppose I couldn't expect anything else. It wasn't as if we knew each other—yet.

'Gossip rags,' I dismissed. 'I'd hardly trust *them.*'

'They report that you're with a different woman every week.'

Irritation bit deep, and I masked it with a tone

of boredom. 'Hardly *every* week. Every other week, perhaps.'

'And now you expect me to believe you want to be married in the—the *biblical* sense, and stay faithful to one woman? To *me*?'

I hesitated for the briefest second—only because I wanted to be sure. I always kept my promises. But it was enough to have her grabbing for her bag and reaching for the door.

'Never mind. That's answer enough. I don't know why you've changed your mind, or why you think having a real marriage—which it *wouldn't* be—is a good idea. Perhaps you like a challenge.' She shook her head. 'Or perhaps I'm a novelty. But I *do* know this. A marriage like you're suggesting would be a disaster for both of us.'

'You don't even *know* what I'm suggesting,' I snapped. I'd had quite enough of her sweeping statements.

'And I don't want to find out,' she retorted.

And then she wrenched open the door and was gone.

I stood there for a moment, breathing hard, my blood firing through me. Perhaps we wouldn't have made it to the bed. But one thing I knew with complete certainty—this wasn't over yet. In fact, it was just beginning.

CHAPTER FIVE

'Daisy, are you listening?'

Maria's voice was playfully exasperated as I tried to refocus on the accounts in front of me.

'Yes, yes—*sygnomi*. I'm a bit distracted, that's all.' I pulled the ledger towards me, intent on seeming businesslike as usual. 'We're well into the black for the first time. That's a very good thing.'

'Yes, and the demand is now greater than the supply. That is how you say it, yes?'

'Yes.'

I smiled, thankful yet again that Maria Petrakis spoke English. She'd been my right-hand woman since I'd come to Amanos, and I could not have started Amanos Textiles without her.

'So we need more spinners and weavers?' I mused.

Amanos Textiles now employed thirty women to spin the turquoise-coloured cloth particular to

the island, thanks to a dye made from local ber-
ries, but clearly we needed more.

The idea had come to me after being on Amanos for a few weeks. I was feeling bored with
my sudden and unexpected freedom. I'd worked
my whole life—cleaning houses with my grandmother from the time I was eight, and then working after-school jobs through my teens and a stint
at a local college in Kentucky. I was so used to
hard work I realised I didn't know how else to
be, and idleness started to feel like anathema.

Besides, after exploring Amanos I'd realised
that employment was low and that the blue cloth
I saw the women wearing was gorgeous. I didn't
know much about fashion or style, but I'd always
known about fabric. My grandmother had taught
me to both quilt and sew, and I'd made my own
clothes since I was twelve.

I'd started small, putting some of the money
Matteo had deposited into my account into starting up a local business employing women who
spun and wove cloth to sell in towns and cities
around Greece. I'd invested the rest, as I'd told
him, and lived off the interest.

Maria, who had made my acquaintance early
on, when I'd got lost on my way to the island's

only village, had been invaluable, and within a year we had several buyers in Athens who were interested in sustaining a local economy and using the blue cloth for their fashions.

It had felt good to use some of the money from Matteo for such a purpose, and Maria had handled the buying side of it—which had been mostly done online anyway. In three years I'd never had to leave the island…until I'd gone in search of Matteo.

Matteo.

His name sent a ripple of…*something*… through me. I was afraid it might be longing. For the last week I'd been going over his offer of a real marriage and half wondering why I'd turned it down. Did I *really* think Mr Right was going to amble along one day? And what about when our marriage was annulled? My life was on Amanos now, wrapped up in this business. I hated the idea of starting over somewhere new, where once again I'd be anonymous and alone.

I was hardly going to find a husband on Amanos, though, and in any case I was already married.

'Daisy?' Maria prompted again. 'Your head is in the sky!'

'You mean the clouds.' I smiled and sighed. 'Sorry…just thinking.'

'You have been "just thinking" since you returned from Athens,' Maria returned shrewdly.

I hadn't told her I'd gone looking for Matteo, but I suspected she'd guessed. She knew about the nature of my marriage and had always been pragmatic about it.

'Yes…' I let out a breath. 'Yes, I have.'

'And what have you been thinking about? Kyrie Dias?'

'How did you know?'

She shrugged. 'Who else could it be?'

No one—because I didn't know anyone anywhere, and certainly not in Athens. Still, I made a half-hearted attempt to direct her attention elsewhere.

'I could have been meeting our buyers.'

'Then you would have told me.'

'True.' I drummed my fingers on the table. 'All right—how about this. We need more spinners and weavers, so what if we start a school for young women? To teach them?'

Part of the problem on Amanos was that the old ways were dying out, and young people were moving to the cities for work. It was the same story back in Kentucky; hardly anyone knew how to quilt any more. In some ways life on Amanos was a lot like it had been back in Briar Valley, just the language was different.

'Yes, that could be a good idea—and also perhaps expanding to the neighbouring islands? Kallia is not so far away.'

'No, that's true. That's a good idea.'

'And now you will tell me about Kyrie Dias?'

Maria's eyes glinted, but I shook my head.

'There's nothing to tell.'

Even if I *was* starting to regret my impulsive rejection of Matteo's suggestion. Even if I *was* doubting that anything better would ever come along.

'I think there is,' Maria said as she gathered up the accounts. 'But I will leave you to tell me another day.'

I smiled at her in gratitude and she waved a farewell before heading back to her home in Holki, the island's only village.

Alone, I wandered around the villa I'd called my home for the last three years.

Matteo had been understating things when he'd said the place was comfortable; it was amazing. Two sprawling floors of white stucco with a red terracotta roof, right on the beach, overlooking the aquamarine waters of the Aegean Sea. I had a bedroom bigger than my apartment back in New York, and the kitchen alone was bigger than my grandmother's house back in Kentucky. I also had the use of an exercise room, an outdoor infinity pool, and a gorgeous garden bursting with bougainvillea and hyacinths.

In my time here I'd made only a few changes—I'd added a herb garden outside the kitchen, and personalised the study, making it into the business headquarters of Amanos Textiles.

The main operation of the company still took place in the women's homes, which was how I'd wanted it. I remembered my grandmother hemming clothes in the evenings after work to make a few extra dollars, and I knew how important it was that women were able to work as well as look after their families.

Deciding the best antidote for my restlessness was work, I headed back to the office and pulled up a report on my laptop. One of the women who spun cloth had suggested a new colour for the cloth, a deeper shade of the turquoise, and I had just received a report from a chemist about the possibility of deepening the dye.

A few minutes later the *rat-a-tat* whirring of a helicopter hovering nearby startled me out of my studies. Search and rescue helicopters were fairly common to the area, but I'd never heard one so close.

As I peered out of the picture window of the large lounge my mouth dropped open and my stomach swirled with dread—and more than a little excitement. It wasn't a search and rescue helicopter. It was a private one, with an *A* and an *E* embossed on its side, about to land on the villa's never-used helipad.

It was Matteo.

In three years he'd never come the island. Everyone knew of him, of course, and I'd heard how he'd come in a whirlwind five years ago and bought the place, staying only for a day. Due to his presence on the island—or lack of it—many of the villagers followed him in the news, just as I did, but they'd never seen him.

And now he was here...*for me?*

A thrill ran through me and instinctively I suppressed it. If Matteo suggested his outrageous proposition again I was going to refuse, wasn't I? Surely that was the sensible, sane thing to do.

And yet...

And yet he was here. And that reality undeniably thrilled me.

I watched, my heart starting to pound, as he emerged from the helicopter and started up the path towards the villa. He strode with purpose, dressed as always in an immaculate three-piece suit, looking polished and diamond-hard. And here *I* was in a pair of cut-off shorts and a T-shirt stained with blotches of turquoise dye. I was hardly the epitome of a professional woman, but I supposed that was one of the fringe benefits of working in a cottage industry on a remote island.

I wasn't prepared for visitors...visitors like my husband.

And right now he was coming through the front door.

I'd given her a week. A week to wonder, to wish, to regret. And hopefully to see sense. The week apart from my wife had only lent fire to my resolve to make this marriage real. And now I was on Amanos, ready to make it happen.

I strode through the villa I'd bought five years ago as an investment property, little knowing then how I would need to use it. I didn't really remember its tastefully bland decoration, but something about it felt subtly different. Enhanced.

Was it simply Daisy's presence? Where *was* she?

Then she stepped into the centre of the living room, her face pale, her chin tilted. 'Hello, Matteo.'

I stopped where I stood, taking her in. Even in a pair of ragged shorts and a stained top she looked eminently desirable. Her legs seemed endless, and the wisps of hair escaping her ponytail framed a face that was heart-stopping in its pure loveliness.

How had I not seen her beauty before? Not recognised it on that rainy street in Manhattan? Perhaps I'd become hardened to it, because I was so used to the polished, brittle glamour of the women I usually consorted with. Now that kind of calculated beauty's finish had cracked, and I'd seen the ugliness underneath. Daisy, on the other hand, seemed fresh. Pure and uncomplicated…unlike our marriage.

But that was all about to change.

'What are you doing here?' she asked unsteadily.

'I want you to reconsider my proposal.'

'That's right to the point.'

'I don't see any need to dissemble.'

'Of course not.'

She gave a small smile, which heartened and even moved me—perhaps more than it should.

'One thing I like about you, Matteo. You're honest.'

The last was said on a sigh, but still… At least she liked something.

'That's enough to build a marriage on, don't you think?' I returned lightly.

I glanced around the room, taking in a few throw cushions in vivid turquoise, but otherwise the place seemed unchanged. So she hadn't redecorated ten times, or even once. What had she spent my money on, then?

'Why don't you give me a tour?' I suggested.

'Of your own house?'

'You've been living here and I never have. I'd like to see what you've done with it.'

'Nothing, really.'

But her gaze slid away from mine. She almost looked guilty, and a new wariness stole through me. What was she hiding? She'd said she could pay me back, but her bank account was nearly empty, no matter what she'd said about investments.

Before I outlined the terms of my new proposal, perhaps I should discover just how my possibly errant wife had been spending so much money.

'Still,' I said, a bit more firmly, 'I'd like a tour.'

She shrugged and moved towards the kitchen. 'You know the place as well as I do.'

'Not really. I only visited it once, for a day.'

I glanced into the kitchen, which looked homelier than I remembered, with some colourful pottery scattered around and pots of herbs and flowers on the windowsill.

Daisy glanced at me uncertainly before moving on, through the other rooms downstairs—the dining room, the media room, the library. Everything looked more or less as I remembered.

'And upstairs?' she said, moving towards the stairs.

I followed her, wondering if I'd find dozens of haute couture gowns in her closet. It seemed unlikely, but I'd seen nothing else on the property that she could have spent her money on, and I'd already checked with my sources to see if any investment accounts had been opened in her name. There hadn't been.

I glanced into five pristine and bland bedrooms, uninterested, before Daisy hesitated in front of the master bedroom. My interest was piqued and my blood heated. I could picture us both on that king-sized bed, sprawled and tangled. I could picture it perfectly. And judging from the flush on Daisy's face, she could, as well.

'Shall we…?' I murmured, and wordlessly she nodded and stepped inside.

The room was vast, with a huge picture window overlooking the beach, and the sea sparkling in the distance like a jewel. But the bed was the true centrepiece, canopied and on its own dais, made for romance. For sex. We both stared at it for a long, prickling moment and images danced through my mind. My palms itched to reach for her and draw her towards that soft expanse piled high with pillows in vivid shades of blue.

Abruptly Daisy turned away. 'And the bathroom,' she muttered, nodding towards an en suite bathroom decorated in black-and-white marble, its sunken whirlpool tub and double shower causing me to envisage other, just as delectable scenarios.

The bed, the bath, even on the floor... I could picture us everywhere.

'Very nice,' I murmured, and when I glanced at Daisy I saw she was nibbling at her lip, her cheeks as bright as roses. Was she thinking the same as me, or was she nervous for another reason? I still hadn't figured out where the money had gone, or if she still had it as she claimed, and now I was more than curious. I needed to know.

'There. That's the tour.'

She started walking down the hallway, looking and sounding unaccountably nervous. I walked slowly after her, processing all I'd seen...and hadn't seen.

What has she done with that money?

Then, as we came downstairs, I noticed a room off the front hall that she had not chosen to go into. The study, if I remembered correctly.

'What about that room?'

'Oh, it's a mess...'

'A mess?' My eyes narrowed as I took in her definite jitters. 'What are you hiding from me, Daisy? How have you spent my money?'

Her jaw dropped and her eyes blazed gold

fire. 'Is that what this little tour has been about? You're trying to figure out how I've spent "your" money—which, I'll remind you yet again, is actually mine, as per our agreement. Besides, I told you I could pay it back.'

'I don't know whether to believe you.'

'What—'

'No investments have been made in your name—either Daisy Campbell or Dias.'

'Seriously? You think I *lied*? How stupid do you think I *am*?'

I didn't answer as I strode towards the door and pushed it open. With a sigh, Daisy followed me.

It took me a few seconds to assimilate what I saw and then to make sense of it. The room was clearly in use. The laptop on the desk was open and surrounded by papers. A noticeboard on the wall was covered in messages and schedules and lists. Swathes of fabric in the same shade of blue I'd seen around the house were draped over various surfaces, and above the window there was a sign wrought out of wicker: Amanos Textiles.

I turned to Daisy. 'What *is* this?'

'My office.' She looked at me mutinously.

'Yes, I can see that—but I didn't think you worked.'

'Well, I do.'

Why was she being so recalcitrant? 'What is Amanos Textiles, Daisy?'

'My company.'

I stared at her, incredulous. '*Your* company?'

'Yes—and the investments I've made are in its name, Smarty Pants.'

'I...'

For once I was truly speechless. I couldn't believe she'd just called me Smarty Pants, and neither could I believe that she'd started her own business. She had never said a word about it. I hadn't the faintest clue—and, I realised, I hadn't actually thought her capable of starting her own company, if that was in fact what she'd done.

'*Your* company?' I repeated, and she heard the scepticism in my voice.

'Yes, *my* company. When I arrived in Amanos I noticed the women wore a lovely blue cloth, and I discovered they weave it here, using a dye made from a plant native to the island. I decided it was marketable, and I set up a company to sell the cloth to manufacturers throughout Greece.'

'You did?' I was even more shocked. 'This is what you used my money for?'

'*My* money—and, yes. I used two hundred

thousand to buy proper equipment, looms and vats for the dye, and also to set up the website and hire someone to help. Maria,' she explained. 'She does a lot of the admin, and as a native Greek speaker she has become my right-hand woman. She helped win my first clients. The rest of the money I invested in the company's name and put the interest back into it. We started turning a profit just over a year ago.'

I shook my head slowly. 'Why didn't you tell me any of this?'

'When would I have told you?' she fired back. 'When we were having one of our regular chats?'

'Is this why you've seemed so nervous? You didn't want to tell me?'

She looked down, a lock of her hair falling forward to hide her face. 'I thought you might be cross.'

'Cross?' I was baffled. 'Why?'

'Because you like to be in control, Matteo. Why else would you have me waiting out our marriage on this island? I thought you might resent the fact that I wasn't just sitting here, waiting.'

I tried for a laugh to mask my sudden and surprising hurt. 'You make me sound like some sort of monster.'

'No, just a control freak.' She sighed. 'But the truth is I didn't know how you'd react because I don't actually *know* you.'

Which provided my perfect opening. 'Then let's change that,' I said with a determined smile. 'Starting now.'

CHAPTER SIX

HE WASN'T ANGRY. Even as relief pulsed through me I wondered what I'd been so afraid of. Why should Matteo be angry that I had started my own business—admittedly in his house, and with the money he'd given me? Still, as I'd told him, it was my money. My life. And now that my nerves had passed I realised I was proud of all I'd achieved, and pleased that Matteo knew about it.

Why I should be pleased, I didn't like to think about. It implied that I cared about his opinion, and I knew I shouldn't. Not if I wanted to keep my distance, which had been my first resolve. Now, with Matteo smiling at me, his expression managing to be both easy and determined, I didn't know what I felt.

'You want to get to know me?' I said uncertainly. 'Really?'

'Yes, really. Is that so hard to imagine?'

'Frankly, yes. Your…transactions with women have not been characterised by your getting to know them, at least in anything other than the physical sense.'

'But we're married,' he pointed out. 'And we're going to have a baby together. It's different.'

'We are *not* going to have a baby together,' I retorted.

I didn't know whether to laugh or scream at the arrogance of the man. Even now, after I'd refused him in no uncertain terms, he was completely confident of winning me round. And the trouble was I knew he might.

'For now, why don't we just have a conversation? Spend the afternoon together and see where it leads?'

He raised his eyebrows expectantly and I did my best not to read innuendo into those words. Not to imagine that big bed upstairs with the two of us in it.

'Fine,' I said, knowing I sounded ungracious. 'Since you came all this way.'

'Why don't you show me the village? I don't think I've actually seen it before.'

'All right.'

Against my better judgement I found myself

warming to the idea. I could show Matteo the warehouse where we stored the finished fabrics, and the building where we kept the dye vats. I realised I was looking forward to showing him that I wasn't the pathetic, washed-up waitress with no sense of style or sense that he'd assumed I was. I might not have oodles of confidence when it came to high society or city life, but here on Amanos I knew who I was. Because it was here that I'd found myself.

'Let me just change,' I said, and Matteo inclined his head.

'I will, as well. I imagine things are casual on the island.'

Upstairs, anticipation fizzed through my stomach along with nerves as I flipped through my limited wardrobe, looking for…what? A cute sundress that managed to be both sexy and demure? Something to show Matteo I was a woman with appeal and beauty?

I let out a huff of humourless laughter. I didn't have anything like that in my wardrobe of mostly shorts, jeans, T-shirts and hoodies—and, anyway, I didn't want to doll myself up for Matteo's sake. The only reason he was interested in me was because I was a challenge.

At least that was what I'd told myself over the last week, when I'd been obsessing about his proposition.

I settled on a pair of capris with a loose top in the turquoise linen of Amanos Textiles. Hardly sexy stuff, but I looked nice enough.

Matteo, as usual, looked almost unbearably attractive. Whether he was in a tuxedo, a suit, or, as now, a pair of dark trousers and a grey polo shirt that brought out the vivid colour of his eyes, he was devastating. He devastated *me.*

'Let's go,' I said, trying to keep my voice light, trying not to react to the way Matteo's gaze seemed to burn my skin as he looked at me.

My every nerve ending felt as if it were tingling to life as we strolled the half-mile down the rock-strewn dirt road that led to Holki.

'Why did you buy this place if you were never going to visit?' I asked as we walked along.

'It was meant to be an investment, but in the end it suited my purposes admirably.' He shot me a gleaming glance, all eyes and teeth. 'You've been happy here?'

'Yes.'

It had been a haven when I needed one, and starting Amanos Textiles had been the purpose

I'd longed for. I suppose, in a somewhat round-about way, Matteo had been responsible for both, and the realisation humbled me. Since confronting him in Athens I'd been so focused on his haughty manner, his displeasure in having me disrupt his rules, that I'd forgotten just how much he'd done.

'Thank you,' I added abruptly.

Matteo raised his eyebrows. 'You're thanking me? How novel.'

'I know… I know.' Impulsively, I punched his arm, laughing a little. 'I'm sorry. You have been very kind in providing me with so much—a home, the means to start my own business… Since seeing you face-to-face, I haven't always seemed grateful.'

'Why is that, do you suppose?'

'Because you can be an arrogant so-and-so.'

I could hardly believe we were talking and teasing like this, but it felt nice. My heart was light.

'It's not arrogance when I'm right.'

'Of course not.' I shook my head. 'I'd expect no less from you.'

'At least you expect *something* from me.'

The import of his words had me blushing.

What was he saying, really? That we had the start of something?

I looked away, keeping my gaze on the shimmering, tranquil waters of the sea in the distance. Already I was feeling out of my depth. A few moments of light-hearted conversation was making my heart do cartwheels. Really, I needed to calm down. What *was* it about Matteo Dias that made my head both empty and spin?

The answer was *everything*.

Daisy was surprising me at every turn, and I found I quite liked it. I was still amazed that she'd built her own business from nothing, and I was looking forward to seeing the extent of the operation. I was also looking forward to spending time with her, which was novel. The time I spent with women was almost always in bed.

Yet here we were, Daisy and I—my *wife* and I—strolling along a sunny road. I glanced at her, noting the way the loose top skimmed her curves, the capris emphasised her slender legs. Her hair was loose about her shoulders in soft, golden-brown waves. I imagined if I kissed her right now she'd taste like sunshine.

But I had to stop thinking that way. Today's little jaunt, pleasant as it was, had a purpose—and that was to prove to my bride that she belonged to me. I would not let myself forget that for a moment.

'So what are the top ten sights of Holki?' I asked as the village with its whitewashed buildings and narrow, cobbled streets came into view.

Daisy threw me a laughing glance. 'I'm not sure there's ten total, never mind at the top.'

'Tell me what I should see first.' I flung my arms wide, enjoying the novelty of a sunny afternoon spent with a beautiful woman, and not in bed.

'Well…' Daisy ducked her head before giving me a shy glance. 'We could visit the workroom and the dyeing areas for Amanos Textiles.'

'You have a workshop? Let's see it, then.'

Over the next few hours my amazement at and my admiration for my wife increased more and more. We toured the workshop—a converted barn that was bright and airy inside, filled with reams of the distinctive blue cloth as well as several industrial-sized tables where women were busy working.

Their eyes rounded when they caught sight of

me, but they were happy for me to see their work. And I was happy to see it too, as well as to listen to Daisy's at first halting and then more confident explanations.

'The women weave the cloth in their homes, because I think it's important that they're able to work from home, where they can still supervise their children, but we dye it in a separate space—because of the mess and the smell—and then finish it off here because we need the space to cut it.'

'And what about your buyers? How did you find those?'

'Online, mostly. I started a website and paid for some advertising. Maria approached a few small, independent clothing retailers—ones we knew supported grass-roots enterprises and cottage industries. It took a while—those one million euros certainly helped provide a cushion.'

'And to think I thought you were redecorating or buying clothes.'

'Over a million euros' worth of clothes?' she exclaimed, looking laughingly appalled. 'And yet I wore that wretched red dress to your ball? Credit me with *some* sense, at least.'

I laughed out loud, enjoying her candid humour even more than the lovely sight of her.

'How did you learn all this?' I couldn't help but ask. 'How did you know what to do?'

Daisy made a little laughing grimace. 'I might not have much fashion sense, but I've worked with cloth all my life. My grandmother taught me to quilt, and I've sewn my own clothes since I was little more than a child.'

'And the business side of things?'

'Maria helped. You'll have to meet her. And I learned along the way—made a lot of mistakes. It's still not a very big business, you know. It hardly rivals Arides Enterprises.'

'It's very impressive.'

'Thank you.'

She smiled and ducked her head, shyly pleased, as we walked out of the workshop into the sunlit square of the village.

'How about lunch?' I suggested, nodding towards the village's one café.

'People will talk if they see us together like this,' she warned.

I shrugged. 'I want them to talk.'

'Matteo...'

'I assume everyone already knows we're married? They will have sussed that out already?'

'Yes, but they also know what kind of marriage it is.'

For some inexplicable reason that annoyed me. It had been my idea, so I knew my reaction was unreasonable, but it still did.

'Then they'll know what kind of marriage it is now,' I said and, taking her hand, I drew her to me and kissed her.

It was meant to be little more than a buss of the lips, but the first strawberry-sweet taste of her had me plundering her mouth for more. As she had before, she opened her mouth under mine, accepting my kiss and returning it, one hand coming up to grasp at my shirt as desire's pistons fired through us both.

In the distance a child laughed, breaking the moment—although only just. Reluctantly I pulled away. Daisy's lips were swollen, her eyes bright.

'Now they'll *really* talk.'

'Let them.'

'Matteo...' She shook her head. 'I haven't agreed, you know. I'm not planning on agreeing to just jump into bed—and *life*—with you.'

We'll see about that, I thought, but wisely did not say. Yet.

'Lunch,' I murmured and, taking her arm, I headed towards the café.

CHAPTER SEVEN

I FOUND IT exceedingly pleasant to sit in the sun at an outside table at the village's café, nibbling souvlaki and drinking red wine, with the *agiorgitiko* grapes indigenous to the region lending it a lush, fruity flavour that was slipping down far too nicely.

I was just a little bit tipsy—which was dangerous. Because the most pleasant part of the afternoon by far was sitting with Matteo, basking in his attention and interest, enjoying his dry humour, as well as enjoying the way his gaze would rest on me in warm approval.

I was like a parched desert that had suddenly encountered cool spring rains and I couldn't soak them up fast enough. Dangerous indeed.

'Tell me about your childhood,' Matteo invited, as if he were fascinated by me, wanting to know every dull detail when the initial rules of our marriage had been to know as little as possible. 'You told me you grew up in Kentucky...?'

When had I told him that? Or had he learned it during his little bout of research?

'Why don't you tell me what you learned on-line?' I threw back, somehow managing to pitch my tone between teasing and slightly piqued.

I felt reckless with wine and attention, daring in a way I almost never was. I couldn't decide if I was flirting or fighting or something in between. I was caught between caution and desire, common sense and a heady recklessness. This was so much fun—and yet it was also more than a little frightening. Matteo was a sexy, charming, *devastating* man…in so many ways. I couldn't let myself forget that.

'Ah, online…' Matteo gave a small smile of acknowledgement. 'Hardly an episode of cyber-stalking. I simply did an internet search of your name in Kentucky, and I came upon a former address for you and your grandmother.'

'Easy enough, I suppose.'

'Yet it told me very little—only that you lived with your grandmother rather than with your parents.'

And yet he'd still been able to surmise so much—the loss of my family and my longing for a child, as if a baby would finally fill that yawning vacuum inside me. Maybe it would, maybe it wouldn't, but I didn't know whether I liked Matteo knowing about it. Knowing about *me.*

I looked away, unsure how to feel about any of this. It was raw and real and nerve-racking to be so vulnerable—especially in front of a man like Matteo, who was still mostly a stranger—but in an odd way it also felt comforting, to be so *known.*

'So...?' Matteo prompted, leaning back in his chair and stretching his long legs out in front of him. 'Take your time...tell me everything. I'm not going anywhere.'

He acknowledged the full intent of his words with a lazy smile. No, he wasn't going anywhere. He was going to stay on Amanos until he got what he wanted—which was what? Me in his bed, as a proper wife, but for how long? And *why*?

'There's not much to say, really,' I answered as I took another sip of the delicious red wine. 'My father was never in the picture and, as I've told you before, my mother died in a car crash when I was eighteen months old.'

She'd been coming home at four in the morning after the graveyard shift at a local diner. A truck driver had fallen asleep at the wheel and veered into her lane. Over in an instant—one life ended, two others changed for ever.

'Yes, you told me that. What I didn't say was that I'm sorry.'

I shrugged. The pain was an old wound that I knew I would always have, but it didn't hurt so much, as long as I didn't probe it too deeply.

'I don't remember my mother, and it's hard to miss someone you never knew.'

'Is it?' Matteo's dark brows drew together as he frowned, a strangely haunted look coming over his face for a moment. 'I'm not sure. I think it can be quite easy.'

Which was an incredibly intriguing statement, but he clearly wasn't going to offer any more, and judging by the sudden closed look drawing his chiselled features together he seemed to regret admitting that much.

'So you and your grandmother lived alone?' he resumed.

'Yes.'

'Were you close?'

I pondered the question for a moment, recalling my evenings alone while my grandmother worked a second shift, or the Saturdays we'd spent together, cleaning someone else's house, working in grim, silent solidarity.

'Out of necessity, I suppose. My grandmother grew up poor and worked all the hours on God's green earth to make ends meet—and then they did, only just. She didn't have time or energy for much more than that.'

'For you?'

His question was just a bit too piquant. 'I didn't feel neglected,' I said, a bit defensively. 'I understood. Of course I did.'

'Even so, you were a child.'

I wasn't sure I'd ever felt like a child. From a young age I'd seen too much of the realities of poverty and hard work and injustice, even as I'd tried desperately not to let them shape me. To keep my optimism and hope even when everything in life insisted I surrender them—white flags to the grinding war of real life.

'I grew up quickly in some ways,' I said after a moment.

And yet in other ways I'd remained terribly naïve, completely inexperienced when it came to certain aspects of life. All I'd known how to do was work hard, and that hadn't been enough to make it in Manhattan. Not by a long shot.

'So, New York…' Matteo said, as if he'd been able to follow my silent train of thought. 'How did you end up there?'

'My granny developed Alzheimer's when I was nineteen. I took care of her until she died, when I was twenty-two.'

I dismissed those three agonising years in a single sentence, and was glad to do so. Who wanted to hear about how dispiriting, how *devastating*, they'd been? Certainly not Matteo.

'When she was gone I realised there wasn't much keeping me in Briar Valley.'

Between caring for my grandmother, taking a few classes at the local college, and holding down two part-time jobs, I hadn't had time to make friends or form ties of any kind, and most people my age had left anyway. It had been a relief to leave the memories behind.

I didn't say any of that to Matteo, however. It was all becoming a bit too pathetic, a bit too 'poor little me'. So I just smiled and reached for my wine. 'I'd always wanted to go to New York. I had dreams of being a singer, once upon a time.'

I tried for insouciance but a sour note entered my voice. That memory hurt too.

'A singer?' Matteo looked properly surprised. 'Now, *that* I really didn't know. So you went to New York to become a star on the stage?'

'Yes—and ended up waitressing instead. A story told a thousand times, I'm sure.'

I was definitely not going to tell him about my awful 'audition' with Chris Dawson, or the terrible words he'd flung at me, and how that experience had led me to my lowest point, which had led me to here. No, I'd talked about myself enough for one day...for one lifetime.

'Anyway, that all went up in smoke, as you know. I sing in the shower these days—if at all.' Hummed was more like it. I'd stopped singing the day Chris Dawson had told me I was deluded about my talent.

You're a talentless nobody, Daisy Campbell, and you always will be.

'Perhaps you'd sing for me?'

Matteo's voice held an undercurrent of sensuality, as if his words had been dipped in dark chocolate.

'I doubt it,' I replied, and my voice was a little too hard to be bright, the way I'd meant it to be. 'Apparently a good voice in Briar Valley, Kentucky, is not a good voice in New York or even anywhere else.'

Matteo's eyebrows rose. 'What do you mean?'

'Just that I was disabused of the notion that I was anything special.'

And that was all I was going to say about that. I'd said too much already, exposing a few too many flaws than was either comfortable or wise.

'Anyway, that's all old news and rather dull,' I said, and this time I thought I'd managed the bright tone. 'Tell me about *you*.'

'Not much to tell.'

There could be no ignoring the repressive tone that Matteo adopted like an invisible, iron mantle—I suspected without even realising it. The doors were inexorably swinging shut.

'There must be something.'

I found I was intensely curious about Matteo Dias. All I knew about him was that he was CEO of Arides Enterprises and he'd married to satisfy his grandfather, to whom he was not close. And, of course, that he was considered the sexiest bachelor in Greece, if not all of Europe, and women fawned and fell at his feet.

But did he have parents? Siblings? Friends?

Hobbies or quirks or funny stories? Birthmarks or scars or hidden talents?

If our marriage turned real would I find out?

'What about your family?' I persisted. 'All I know is you have a grandfather you don't like very much.'

'Massive understatement, I'm afraid, but he feels the same.' Matteo's smile didn't look like a smile.

'What about your parents? Siblings?'

'My parents are both dead, and have been since I was a baby.'

'I'm sorry—'

'Don't be. Like you, I never knew them.'

Which reminded me of that poignant comment he now seemed to regret making—how it could be easy to miss something you never knew. What did he miss? The love of a parent?

'What about brothers or sisters?' I asked.

A hesitation, and then he admitted with reluctance, 'I have one half-brother. Andreas.'

'Are you close?'

'In a manner of speaking.'

I frowned. 'What does that mean?'

Another hesitation, and I waited, holding my breath, longing to know more. 'He suffered a

TBI—a traumatic brain injury—when he was young. He's never been the same since.'

'Oh, Matteo, that's terrible.'

'For him more than me. Some might say—in fact, *have* said—that it was quite a boon for *me*.'

'What do you mean?'

He shook his head. 'Enough of that. It's an old and boring story.'

Now there could be no disguising the hard finality of his tone. He must have heard it himself, because he smiled—a widening of his mouth, a gleaming of his teeth—but it looked like nothing more than a charade, and that unsettled me.

How much of this afternoon had been an act? Why was he so reluctant to part with even minor details about his life?

'Anyway,' he resumed, in a *case closed* sort of voice, 'we have more important things to discuss.'

'Such as?'

'Our marriage.'

His smile sharpened to a point, his eyes glinting like metal. My stomach tightened with both anticipation and nerves. Was I ready to talk about this? After my scornful and complete refusal of his proposition a week ago, could I *really* be considering it now, even in the smallest degree?

I was. Heaven help me, I was. And I feared there was nothing *small* about it.

'All right,' I said, lifting my chin as I met his glinting gaze with what I hoped was a steady one of my own. 'Let's talk.'

Triumph surged through me as I held Daisy's gaze. *I had her.* We hadn't even talked about the details yet, but I knew I had her. It was just a matter of time.

'So, you told me I didn't know what a real marriage with you would look like,' she said, her voice firm, her gaze holding mine without a flicker.

She was, I suspected, a little tipsy, and it had given her a certain Dutch courage which I didn't mind.

'So tell me. What *would* it look like?'

'What would you *want* it to look like?'

'You're prevaricating.'

I was, but I wasn't about to admit it. 'Not at all. I'm interested in your thoughts.'

'Since when?'

Now her confidence was turning aggressive. I didn't think I liked that as much.

'Since I decided I wanted to make our marriage real.'

'Which was when?' She shook her head slowly. 'Because the thing is, Matteo, I'm not sure I believe that you actually do.'

'You don't believe me?' I stared at her incredulously. 'Why on earth would I come all this way, go to all this effort, if I wasn't serious?'

She shrugged, her gaze sliding away from mine. 'I don't know. Because you see me as a challenge? Or perhaps a novelty?'

She turned back to me, eyes flashing.

'Neither is a good reason for going the distance with someone—and I'm *not* talking about physically.' A rose-pink blush tinted her cheeks. 'Or at least not just physically.'

I tried not to feel offended by her words and failed. Did she honestly think me so shallow that I would pursue marriage simply because it felt like a challenge? I was almost tempted to inform her that I'd had plenty of such *challenges*, and she was not so much of one as she seemed to think. But I didn't. Because it wasn't strictly true. The women I'd been with had not been challenges at all—except perhaps in the challenge not to have me become bored.

Daisy was as different from them as the sun was from the rain-swept sea—so did that mean she *was* a challenge? In the space of a few seconds I'd managed to tie myself in mental knots, and I didn't like that, either.

'You don't even have a response?' Daisy shook her head, disappointment darkening her eyes to the colour of whisky. 'Figures.'

'Figures?' I'd most certainly had enough of her insults. 'And what is *that* supposed to mean?'

'That I'm right.'

'You sound disappointed.' Which was something, at least. Vindication would have been much harder to stomach. 'I thought we were going to talk about the particulars of our marriage, not whether my intentions were honourable or not—although I have to confess, they must *be* honourable, because we're talking about marriage.'

'We're already married.'

'You know what I mean.'

'Fine.' She folded her arms under her bosom, highlighting that asset to becoming effect. 'What *are* the particulars?'

'I asked you first what you would expect from a marriage such as ours.'

'Ah, yes, that's where we started. With your prevarication. You're afraid that I'll be completely appalled by what you expect, and how it differs from what *I* expect, so you want to suit your answers to my concerns. But of course you don't know what they are.'

There was entirely too much truth in that statement. 'I'm merely curious.'

'So am I. So perhaps I should tell you what I think *you* expect.'

Her eyes and her smile both gleamed, and I wondered if she was actually enjoying this unexpected repartee. There was a prickle to her, as well as a bite. I think she liked baiting me, the she-devil, but I knew I had the ability to hurt her, and I found I didn't like that at all. That was one power I did not wish to have.

'Fine. Tell me what I expect.'

Daisy leaned back in her chair, her lids dropping to half mast as she surveyed me with a sleepy consideration I found beguiling. I arranged my features into a neutral expression of bland interest and waited for what I suspected would be a damning verdict.

'First off, you want a wife in your bed. It seems you're a man of voracious appetite in that regard, so I imagine you want a wife in your bed with some regularity.'

Her words alone were enough to make me shift in my seat, desire arrowing through me in piercing, uncomfortable points.

In my bed with some regularity.

Yes, indeed—I could get on board with that.

'And I think she'd need some imagination.'

Colour pinkened her cheeks but she didn't look away. Now it was getting interesting. I didn't think she'd be saying any of this if she hadn't had several glasses of wine.

'Some,' I agreed, inclining my head. 'But I am not a man of wild tastes.' I smiled, letting my gaze linger. 'Not *too* wild, at any rate.'

Now she did look away, shaking her head. 'I'm afraid I have very little of either experience or imagination when it comes to…that.'

'I'm sure you're eminently teachable.'

'That's not the point I'm trying to make, Matteo.' She turned back to me, her face fiery. 'That's not it at all.'

'Then what is?' I asked with equanimity.

'That you don't want anything else. You want

a wife when it suits you, and you definitely don't want one when it doesn't.'

'That is not true.'

'You don't even *know* me. This is the first time we've spent any time together. Why on earth would you decide to be married to me—really married? Have you decided you want a baby after all?'

'Actually, yes. As I told you, I need an heir.'

'An *heir*? What is this? The fourteenth century?'

'No, it's the twenty-first—in a country that honours the concept of family.'

'And yet until I mentioned wanting a family myself you didn't seem too bothered by the notion. You certainly hadn't thought of babies.'

'I changed my mind.'

I stared at her flushed face, and her eyes glittering with anger, and wondered how our pleasant afternoon had morphed into this. She was angry, and I hadn't expected her to be. I don't think she had either.

'Just like that,' she said after a moment, deflating a little.

'I gave it some thought, I assure you.'

'Not very much.'

'You underestimate me.' Now I was getting angry as well. 'So many assumptions, Daisy.'

'Then maybe it's time you *tell* me what you want from a wife, because you seem remarkably reluctant to do so.'

Which was true—simply because I didn't want to broach the dreaded and unfortunate subject of love. I had no intention of falling in love with Daisy, and I knew I needed to be upfront about that from the start if a marriage of any kind between us was going to work. Yet I suspected saying so would back Daisy into a corner from which it would be very difficult to prise her.

'Very well,' I said. 'I'll tell you what I would like from a wife. I would like a woman who will be a loving mother to my child and a willing partner in and out of bed.'

Her eyes widened, as if she hadn't expected that much.

'And I want someone I can have by my side at the various events and functions I must attend for work.'

As I said it I realised I meant it. It had become tedious, trying to find a suitable woman to accompany me to this or that. Imagine the ease of always having the same woman. *Daisy.*

'And you think *I'm* that woman?' she asked incredulously. 'Matteo, I grew up dirt-poor in the backwoods of Kentucky. You've seen for yourself how little dress style I have. If I went to those types of events I'd only embarrass you.'

For some reason that angered me. 'You would not embarrass me, Daisy.'

I almost told her that her background was not as insalubrious as my own, but I held my tongue. There was no need for me to part with such details now. She would undoubtedly—and unfortunately—learn them in time.

'I can hire a personal stylist for you,' I said instead. 'Such things are easily learned.'

'So is that it?' she asked after a moment. 'A wife in your bed and on your arm?'

'You make it sound so little.'

'It's more than I expected, I suppose.' She rested her chin in her hand, her expression turning distant. 'But it's not enough.'

Ah, here we were at the nub of the matter. Love—that nebulous, unnecessary emotion, so hard to pin down, so pointless to pursue. I should know.

'I presume you're talking about love?' I said, in a tone a touch away from a bored drawl.

'Yes, and I can tell you're not impressed.'

'Not particularly—but what *is* love, anyway, Daisy? You said you haven't ever known it, and you also said you can't miss what you've never known.' I smiled, proud of my neat logic. 'So if you had a marriage without love who's to say it wouldn't work? That it wouldn't be good, or even wonderful?'

CHAPTER EIGHT

MATTEO WAS SMILING at me like the proverbial cat that got the cream, and I wasn't sure how to respond. My head felt fuzzy from the sun and the wine, and I had a sinking feeling I wasn't going to win this argument.

Yes, I had said those things, and put together they made a compelling argument, but it was one I was still reluctant to endorse.

'What do you have against love?' I asked.

He shrugged. 'Nothing against it, per se. I'm just not sure it's worth the paper it *isn't* written on.'

I frowned, wishing I had more of my sense about me. I'd drunk and said and thought too much today. I didn't know where I was any more in regard to Matteo or marriage. I'd spent the last two hours gazing upon his impressive form, wondering if the skin at the open neck of his shirt would feel as sun-warmed and smooth as it looked, even as I said too much about myself and learned far too little about him.

'What is that supposed to mean?' I asked.

'What is love, Daisy?'

He leaned forward, with the light of a zealot in his eyes. He believed whatever he was about to say, I realised with a plunging sensation. Which meant he *didn't* believe in love.

'It's an emotion, I suppose,' I answered after a moment, when I realised Matteo was waiting for a reply.

'Exactly. An emotion. And should we trust our emotions, fleeting as they are? Angry one minute, sad the next, happy when the sun is shining, sad when it rains?'

'Not everyone is such a flibbertigibbet as that.'

'Flibbertigibbet? I like that. But my point remains the same.'

'Love is more than an emotion, then,' I argued, again wishing I had my wits about me. 'It's an… an action. A commitment.'

'No, *marriage* is a commitment. A sacred vow.'

I rolled my eyes. 'Now you're coming out with the sacred stuff—when you fully intended to have our marriage annulled as soon as it suited you?'

'This would be different, and you know it.'

Yes, I did know it—but would it be different enough?

On one hand, it felt as if Matteo was offering me almost everything I wanted—companionship, a child, lifelong security, and of course physical pleasure. I was quite sure he could deliver on *that*.

But the flipside was dark indeed…because with all those lovely things came frustration, fear, hurt, and the very real danger of falling in love with someone who had no intention or even the ability to fall in love with me.

Matteo leaned back in his chair. 'I have a proposal,' he announced.

'Another one?'

'A trial, if you like. I have two events in the next few weeks—a charity gala in Paris and the opening of my new hotel in the Caribbean. Why don't you come with me to both? See how you like it?'

I goggled at him. 'Are you serious?'

'Of course. Why do you find that so difficult to believe?'

'Because the last time I saw you in public you were less than pleased—'

'I've told you. I've changed. Why can't you believe that?'

Because on a fundamental level I knew Matteo hadn't changed at all. Perhaps a few spots had been sloughed off the leopard, but he was still a dangerous predator and always would be.

'I need to be on Amanos for work...'

'You mentioned a right-hand woman? I'm sure she is more than capable of managing things for a few weeks.'

Which was true, but still I resisted—out of fear as well as too strong a temptation.

'I wouldn't even know how to *be* at places like that, Matteo. I really don't think I'm the right woman for this.'

'You're the right woman because I say you are. You're my wife, Daisy. And surely our marriage deserves a chance, at least? You don't even know what you're refusing.'

I took a deep breath. A few weeks. It didn't seem like a very long time. 'And what would happen during these two weeks? Besides me being on your arm at parties?'

His eyes and teeth both gleamed. 'Whatever you want to.'

'And if I say no after the two weeks you'll drop

the whole notion? You won't persist in this idea of a real marriage?' It pained me a little to make that addendum. In two weeks I might never see Matteo again.

Matteo hesitated for a millisecond, and then he nodded. 'Yes.'

I believed him—because I could tell it cost him to promise that. He was a man who took his promises seriously, never mind that he'd married for convenience.

'And what about the…the physical side of things?'

'I'm not going to force you into my bed, if that's what you mean.'

The implication being that he wouldn't need to. I could tell that by both his tone and smile. And I was afraid he was right.

How could I be so weak? How could I want so much and yet at the same time know it was so little?

'I don't know…' I hedged.

The thought of appearing on Matteo's arm, facing all those spiteful society types, was frankly terrifying—and that was without considering the other terrifying part of the equation: being alone with Matteo. Night after night. Temptation after temptation.

'I really don't think I'm the right person for this.'

'And I'm telling you, you are. This deserves a trial, Daisy. *We* do. Two weeks. It's not very much to ask.'

I gazed at him uncertainly as his silvery gaze bored into mine. 'When you put it like that...'

'You are capable of so much more than you seem to think you are. You've worked hard all your life, you moved to a strange city by yourself, you accepted a deal most women would be wary of, moved to a new country and made the most of it, even building up your own business. Daisy, you can *do* this. You've already done so much.'

The sincerity throbbing in his voice and blazing in his eyes brought tears to my own. 'Do you really mean that?' I asked in a wobbly voice. No one had ever said such kind things to me—*ever*.

'Yes, I do. Absolutely.'

I believed him—and that was what made me decide. Matteo was right; we deserved two weeks at the very least. He did, and I did as well.

For better or worse.

'All right,' I whispered. 'I'll do it.'

Triumph flashed across Matteo's face like lightning and he rose from the table, snapping his fingers at the waiter for the bill before reaching for my hand. I felt as if I'd just set a juggernaut in motion, and I didn't know whether to leap out of the way or brace myself for impact.

'Excellent. I'll make the necessary preparation and we'll leave for Athens tonight.'

'Tonight? But—'

'The event in Paris is in a few days and there is much to be done.'

'I feel like Eliza Doolittle.'

'Not at all. But perhaps you are Pygmalion's statue and I am going to bring you to life.' His fingers tightened on mine. 'And I will enjoy doing so, I promise you.'

Yes, I wondered, *but would I?*

I barely had time to think through that question, for the juggernaut continued to grow in strength and speed.

Within minutes of returning to the villa Matteo was on the phone, barking out orders, arranging I knew not what.

I retreated to my study to make my own arrangements. Maria was more than happy to take the helm of Amanos Textiles for a bit, as I'd known she would be.

'You're going away with Kyrie Dias?' Her voice brimmed with excitement. 'He's so handsome, Daisy—'

'Yes...'

Now that it was becoming reality I felt the leaden weight of dread and fear in my stomach. I really didn't know if I was up for this. Any of it.

'It's just for a few weeks...for a business matter.'

As dear a friend as Maria had become, I wasn't in the habit of baring my soul to anyone—and Matteo's suggestion of a trial felt like something too strange and sacred to share. I didn't need to, anyway. Maria had arrived at the whole picture by herself.

'Just a business matter?' she echoed rather gleefully. 'Of course.'

It didn't take very long for me to hand over all the pressing matters to Maria, and soon I drifted upstairs, tinglingly conscious of Matteo's presence in the house even though I didn't know what room he was in.

I supposed I should pack, but one look at my rows of T-shirts and jeans made me realise I had absolutely nothing suitable for a party in Paris and a weekend at a luxury hotel in the Caribbean.

What was I doing? Why had I agreed to this?

'Because, as usual, when I get too near Matteo I cease to think,' I answered myself out loud.

'Ah, here is my lovely bride.'

I whirled around to see Matteo lounging in the doorway, a satisfied smile on his face. Had he heard what I said? I sincerely hoped not.

'Are you ready?'

'Ready?' I repeated, thinking, *Not in the slightest*. 'For what, precisely?'

'To leave. My helicopter is waiting. We'll have dinner in Athens.'

I swallowed. Hard. 'Matteo, I'm not sure if I—'

'Now, now, no cold feet,' he admonished. 'This is happening. You agreed.'

'I haven't packed—'

'You don't need to pack. Everything will be provided for you. Now, come.'

He turned away, leaving me gaping. *Just like that?*

'On second thought,' he said, glancing back at me, 'you should bring a sweater. It's chilly at night still.' His smile was positively wolfish. 'But, trust me, *glykia mou*, that's all you need.'

I was feeling entirely pleased as I settled back in the seat and the helicopter began to lift from its landing pad. The island of Amanos was spread out before us in a tableau of rocky hills and dusty olive groves, with the blue-green of the Aegean touching the horizon. Across from me Daisy peered out of the window, her face pale with anxiety even as excitement sparkled in her eyes.

Such a lovely tangle of contradictions—fear and joy, excitement and nerves. I appreciated her uncertainty, considering what lay ahead, but I was even more pleased by the shy glances she kept slipping me when she thought I wasn't looking. Whatever she might tell herself, my wife wanted to be here.

I'd won.

Of course, it wasn't actually *about* winning, I reminded myself, conscious that Daisy had been making that exact point. She wasn't a challenge or a novelty, as she'd claimed; she was both, as well as much more. She was my wife, and I had no regrets about having her here with me. No regrets at all.

Briefly my mind flicked back to that necessary but uncomfortable conversation about love. I thought I'd done a fairly good job of showing her the ephemeral nature of such emotions, but of course she would need more convincing.

Still, I was confident she would come to see how pointless it was to hanker after that elusive emotion—a slippery sensation if ever there was one. Love was nothing but an illusion, albeit a powerful one. I'd taught myself not to yearn for it a very long time ago, out of necessity. I could teach Daisy the same.

I leaned back, determined to enjoy the short flight to Athens—as well as what would happen afterwards.

The noise of the rotors made it impossible to talk, which was just as well, since I was still processing all I'd learned from the conversation we'd had earlier. I'd talked more with Daisy than I had with any other woman in my life, and while getting to know her hidden strengths and depths had been fascinating, it had also been a bit uncomfortable. It was a burden, knowing so much about someone, and one I was hesitant to bear.

My life, similar to Daisy's, has been one of isolation. When you don't care about people, they can't hurt you. Cut them off first, so they can't cut you—that had been my motto from early on. I'd chosen to despise my grandfather, because then his contempt and loathing would roll off me. The only person I'd ever truly cared about was Andreas, and that was the simplest and easiest thing in my life, because of who he was. But caring about Daisy…

Of course, that wasn't going to happen. And, more importantly, she wasn't going to care about me—never mind actually *love* me. I wouldn't let her.

An hour later the helicopter touched down outside Athens, where a limo was waiting to escort us to my penthouse apartment off Syntagma Square. Daisy followed me, wide-eyed and silent, from helicopter to limo to home. By the time we stepped into the massive marble-lined foyer it was nearing nine o'clock and I could see she was exhausted.

'Why don't you shower and change?' I suggested. 'I'll order something for us to eat.'

She glanced around the apartment, with its chrome and leather furnishings, modern artwork and gleaming marble floors. 'What is this place?'

I looked at her in surprise. 'My home. One of them, anyway.'

She shook her head slowly, but didn't say anything else.

'The bedroom is on the left. There are clothes you can wear in one of the closets.'

Wordlessly she walked down the hall and disappeared into the bedroom, leaving me wondering, a touch uneasily, what she was thinking. Was she simply overawed by the opulence of my lifestyle? Even though she'd been living in a luxurious villa for the last three years, it was obvious to see that her tastes were simple.

I realised I was looking forward to showering her with gifts, spoiling her with things she'd never possessed or experienced before. I was looking forward to it very much indeed.

A few minutes later I strolled into the bedroom, peeling off my shirt and unbuckling my trousers. I wanted a hot shower myself, as well as to remind my shy bride that we were man and wife, even if she wanted to act as if we weren't.

'What are you *doing*?'

Daisy's voice came out in a squeak as she stood in the doorway of the bathroom, a towel clutched around her curvy form, her eyes wide with shocked outrage even as her gaze roved up and down my mostly naked form, lingering on my chest before moving back to my face.

'Stripping,' I answered succinctly. 'I'm intending to use the shower after you.'

'Can't you use another one?'

The squeaking persisted, as did the gaze-roving. I didn't mind either. She looked lovely, with her hair in damp tangles around her flushed face, the towel leaving little—and yet so much—to my overactive imagination.

'There isn't one.'

'This place has only one bathroom?'

'It's my private home. I only need one bathroom.'

And quite a bathroom it was, with a sunken tub, a double shower, and a sauna room. Perhaps, eventually, we would try out all three…

'But you said…' Her voice quivered, along with her chin.

'That I wouldn't force you to do anything you didn't want to do.' I read her uncertain expression perfectly. 'Of course I won't. What kind of man do you think I am?'

'One who struts naked into my bedroom!'

Ah, the maidenly outrage. 'I'm not strutting, and this is not *your* bedroom. It's *ours*.' I took satisfaction in saying that word.

'Surely this place has a guest bedroom?'

'No, it does not. I've never had a guest who required a separate bedroom.'

'Of course you haven't.'

She hitched her slipping towel higher, affording me a glimpse of the tops of her breasts before she knotted the towel with firm decision.

'So you expect us to share a bedroom? A bed?'

I nodded towards the king-sized bed. 'It looks big enough to me.'

'Of course it does.'

She bit her lip, and I wondered if she was waiting for me to be ridiculously gallant enough to offer to sleep on the sofa. I wouldn't. I'd promised not to touch her—not that I'd keep my distance at all times.

'Can you at least give me a little privacy while I get dressed?' she demanded in a quavering voice, and I gave a gracious nod.

'Of course. I'll take a shower.'

After I emerged from the shower and dressed I found Daisy curled up in the corner of a white leather sofa in the living room, clearly dressed in the most modest clothes she could find, staring out at the starry night, her expression drawn in thought.

'The food should be here shortly,' I told her, and she nodded without looking at me. I regarded her for a moment, wondering what was bothering her. 'You found something to wear, I see.'

'Who do the clothes belong to?'

Ah, was she jealous? The thought pleased me. 'No one. I had them delivered today—for you. Tomorrow I've arranged for several stylists and beauticians to come directly to our hotel in Paris.'

She gave another nod, without so much as a glance. I was starting to feel a bit irritated, or perhaps it was something more than that.

'What is it?' I asked.

Finally her gaze slid to mine, as quiet as the rest of her. 'Nothing.'

'Why are you so…?' *Sad?* I stopped before I said the word—because why did I care? I had never once before been attentive or attuned to a woman's emotions. The fact that Daisy's affected mine so significantly was both worrisome and annoying.

'Why am I so what?'

'Never mind.' I ran my fingers through my damp hair as I headed towards the kitchen for a beer. 'It doesn't matter.'

Still, her quiet stillness, the definite sorrow emanating from her, persisted all evening—and persisted in irritating and unsettling me. *Don't care*, I instructed myself, frustrated that I even had to issue such a directive. When had I ever had to before?

'What's wrong?' I burst out, after we'd eaten a mostly silent meal and Daisy had announced her intention to go to bed.

'Nothing's wrong.'

'You've been looking long-faced all evening.'

'This feels a bit strange, that's all.'

'Strange can be good.'

'And it can also be bad. Or just…strange.' She shook her head. 'Why do you care, Matteo?'

Exactly. 'I don't,' I said shortly. 'But it's not very entertaining, sitting with someone who looks as sour as a pint of old milk.'

'What a lovely comparison,' she snapped, her ire rising—which was debatably better than her melancholy mood. 'I didn't realise it was my job to entertain you.'

'That's not what I meant,' I said in exasperation. But she was already gone, the bedroom door shutting smartly behind her.

CHAPTER NINE

I LAY IN THE DARK, staring up at the ceiling, feeling entirely out of sorts. I'd known it would be strange…coming here, being with Matteo…but I hadn't been prepared for *how* strange—or, more alarmingly, how the yearning in me would feel like an empty well that desperately needed filling.

This afternoon in the sunshine felt like a very long time ago, rather than just a few hours. Coming to this sterile, stately apartment had reminded me just how much of a blank slate Matteo was—a deliberately blank state, with him not wanting to be known, never mind loved. And of course I didn't love him. Because I couldn't even get to know him.

And yet I still yearned. I saw glimpses of his kindness, felt the sun-warmed kiss of his approval, and my heart turned right over as my hopes started to soar. Those glimpses were so little, and yet somehow they almost seemed enough, and that scared me. I'd always known I wanted love. I'd felt that hunger and I'd made it a hope, a happiness.

One day...

Accepting Matteo's proposal three years ago had put that hope on hold, naturally, but it hadn't killed it. Even though life had done its best to beat it out of me, I'd held on to it all along. Against all odds. Against all reason.

One day...

And now here I was, letting that treacherous little seedling unfurl inside me and start to grow, even though I knew it shouldn't. It *absolutely* shouldn't. Because Matteo Dias, husband or not, was just about the last person who would ever love me. And more fool me if I loved him anyway, or tried to, simply because he paid me some scant attention.

I sighed heavily, turning over on my side, knowing sleep would be a long time coming as my thoughts continued their crazy dance of *no, you shouldn't* and *if only he did*, with no answers in sight except the obvious one.

Be sensible, Daisy. Keep your head squarely on your shoulders for two weeks and then walk away!

Or rather, run.

I tensed as I heard the door click open, and then the quiet, slithery sound of clothes being shed as Matteo came into the room and began to undress. First the clink of his belt buckle and then the purr of his zipper, as loud as a car engine in the thick silence of the darkened room.

My heart lurched into my throat and my whole body tingled. Not with fear or nervousness, but with what I knew—much to my shame as well as my excitement—was anticipation. Electric, erotic anticipation.

I remained entirely still, determined to act as if I were asleep, even as tension twanged through every muscle and sinew and my nerve endings sizzled. The bed had to be at least five feet wide. As Matteo had said, there was plenty of space for both of us…which was more disappointment than not.

And yet…*a bed*. A bed that we were sharing. I'd never shared a bed with anyone but my grandmother before. What if we accidentally rolled into one another? What if he reached for me in his sleep? What if…?

The mattress dipped under Matteo's weight and the cedar-scented musk of him assaulted my senses and battered them down. Longing swept through me like a river in full flood, and still I remained rigid as he made himself comfortable, turning over his pillow before settling down with a sigh as if he hadn't a care in the world. As if he wasn't on fire the way I was.

The silence stretched on…and on. I couldn't so much as twitch a finger, and my eyes felt gritty with fatigue as my body twanged and twanged— a violin longing for the touch of a bow. I was never going to go to sleep. I was going to *combust*.

'Relax, Daisy,' Matteo said, amusement lacing his words like rich honey.

Clearly he hadn't fallen for my fake sleep routine, such as it was.

'I said I wouldn't touch you and I meant it. You can sleep safely.'

Which I supposed was meant to be reassuring, but it tasted like disappointment. I did my best to relax—not that he'd be able to notice. The night was going to be very long.

Soon enough Matteo's breathing evened and deepened; the man had gone to sleep while I lay there tense and aching and so very *aware*. It was insufferable that he could be so little tempted while I was so much. The ache in me was intensifying with every breath I took. I wanted to nestle closer into the warm, solid curve of his shoulder and breathe in that manly, woodsy scent. I wanted to trail my fingers along the stubble of his hard jaw, tilt my head up for the touch of his lips on mine, deepen the kiss as he angled his head and slanted his mouth…

Stop it, Daisy. Stop it right now.

But already my mind was racing down rabbit trails, finding ways to justify snuggling just a little bit closer—or, if I was jarringly honest, more than a little. I'd been lonely all my life in one way or another, hoping for love without knowing how to look. What if this was the closest I ever got? Just what was I keeping my heart—my body—safe for?

Suddenly it seemed like a nonsensical idea, this instinct of mine to self-protect, to throw up invisible barriers where there needed to be none. If I was trying to keep myself from getting hurt, surely it was already a lost cause?

And in the meantime…

I rolled over onto my side, my heart beating like a drum, blood pounding in my ears. I faced Matteo, barely making out his features in the dark, yet sensing him in every way possible. If

I reached my hand out I could touch his chest, feel his heart thud beneath my palm, the sculpted muscles rigid against my fingers. If I angled my head a little I could almost brush my lips against his. Already I recalled their velvety softness, the honeyed taste of him, and the way he took control of a kiss, made me drown in it. In *him*.

Then Matteo muttered under his breath, a garbled sound of discontent, and I stilled. Was he awake after all?

Embarrassment scorched through me, making my heart beat even harder. Was he laughing at me and the way I was wiggling my way across the bed to him, so blatantly and humiliatingly obvious in my intentions?

He muttered again, in Greek, and it took me a moment to make out the words.

'Ochi...ochi...parakalo...'

No...no...please.

What on earth...? I stilled, straining to hear the words muttered under his breath, sounding like broken pleas.

'Ochi...' And then, agonised, the words were ripped from him, *'Mi...mi!'*

Don't...don't!

'Matteo...'

Whatever was going on in his mind it was clearly terrible, and I couldn't help but try to comfort him. The desire that had been rushing through me had been replaced by an even deeper concern.

Tentatively I laid one hand on his shoulder, felt his skin hot and silky beneath my touch. 'Matteo, wake up. You're dreaming. It's just a dream.'

His body jerked under my hand and still he muttered.

'Matteo.'

I tried to give his shoulder a little shake, even though it felt like moving granite. Then his eyes opened, their silver depths blazing into mine, branding me. I stilled, trapped by his hard, metallic gaze, and then in one fast, fluid motion he rolled on top of me, pinning me beneath him—a movement not of desire, but defence.

I pressed my hands against his shoulders, afraid of what he might do in his sleep-addled state. 'Matteo… Matteo…it's me. Daisy.'

I knew he wasn't really awake. His gaze was piercing and yet unfocused, his body trapping mine, hard and hot.

'Matteo! You were dreaming!'

Shocked, I saw the silvery tracks of tears glistening on his cheeks. It was so unexpected I couldn't make sense of it at first. Matteo...*crying?*

I gentled my voice. 'Matteo, it was a nightmare. Just a nightmare. It's all right now, I promise.'

For a long moment he stared down at me, his body poised over mine, and then abruptly, muttering a curse, he rolled off me. My breath came out in a shuddering gasp, the intensity of the moment making my limbs feel weak, my heart stutter in my chest.

I scooted into a sitting position. Matteo was sitting on the edge of the bed, his tautly muscled back to me, and the tension in the room was thick enough to taste.

'Matteo,' I said quietly, trying to keep both my voice and body from shaking, 'what happened? What were you dreaming about?'

'I wasn't dreaming.' His voice came out terse, almost angry, in an instant rejection of the obvious.

I was half tempted to drop it, since he sounded so fierce, but I knew I couldn't. 'You were asleep. You were muttering something...'

'No, I wasn't.' Again, utter refusal of the obvious.

Once more he'd drawn that invisible iron mantle around him like a cloak and there was no getting past it. He rose swiftly and stalked to the bathroom, closing the door behind him with a loud click.

I sat there baffled, uncertain, a little bit afraid and a lot curious. Whatever he said now, he *had* been dreaming, and it had *not* been a good dream. Yet he seemed like the last man on earth who would succumb to the terror of a nightmare.

My husband, I realised, had hidden depths. As blank a slate as he wanted to appear, as much as he pulled that wretched mantle around him, he wasn't unknowable. He had memories and dreams, even hopes and fears, just like anyone else. He just didn't want me to know about them.

A short while ago that would have quelled my hopes for our supposedly *real* marriage quite significantly, but now, for some contrary reason, it buoyed them higher. Glimpsing that moment of unintended vulnerability had cracked open Matteo's heart...as well as my own.

Matteo had secrets...and perhaps if I got to know them I would be able to understand this complex, contrary man I had married. Perhaps I would learn to love him and he would learn to let me.

I stared grimly at my reflection. Sweat beaded my brow and the aftershocks of that wretched nightmare were still rippling through me. The suffocating darkness, the tiny space, the snick of the key in the lock—and then the hours. Oh, the hours. It had been endless...

Still, I had survived, and I'd certainly moved on. I hadn't had that stupid dream since I was a child. Why on earth had I had it now, the first night I'd shared my bed with Daisy?

Turning on the water, I splashed my face, furious with myself for being so weak. I thought of the gentle pity in Daisy's voice and everything in me cringed. This was *not* how our marriage was meant to work.

Taking a deep breath, I stared hard at myself in the mirror. I needed to get control of the situation immediately, because I could not countenance another episode such as the one I'd just experienced. Daisy could not create a weakness or a need in me; her artless ways could not crack open anything—and certainly not memories of the needy child I'd once been, begging for love when there was absolutely none to be had.

Love was an illusion. I'd had to inform Daisy of that fact. But it seemed I needed reminding as well—which was aggravating in the extreme. All along I'd been confident of managing Daisy, without realising that I needed to manage myself as well.

I turned from the mirror, and the hard blankness in my eyes, and went back into the bedroom. Daisy was curled up on her side, knees tucked up, hair spread across the pillow. She was silent, but I could tell from her wary stillness that she was awake.

For a second, no more, I thought about saying something. Touching her, even. Her curled-up position made me think of something wounded, bracing itself for more pain. And yet *I* was the one who'd had the wretched nightmare.

She didn't move as I got into bed, her back still to me. I rolled onto my side away from her, everything in me tense and aching. Neither of us spoke, and I told myself that was good thing. It had to be.

Still, sleep eluded me, and the moon slanted silver shadows across the floor as I lay there, tense and angry, memories lapping at my senses in a way I hated.

Not just the old nightmare of the locked cupboard, which had been a staple of my sleep for several years of my childhood, but of other things. My grandfather's complete and utter ignoring of me, stepping around me as if I were genuinely invisible, no matter how much I tried not to be…until he needed me. And Eleni…the spectre of my childhood…with her screwed-up face, her voice hissing at me like a snake.

You're worthless…

She hadn't been telling me anything I didn't already know by heart.

I forced the memories away by a sheer, gritty act of will and tried to think of something else instead. Something positive. Andreas, smiling at me with his grin of pure joy. Daisy, looking at me from under her lashes this afternoon, her lips curving so sweetly…

But those memories disturbed me as well, because I wasn't used to needing people to make me happy. Needing anyone for anything. I'd trained myself not to, and yet here I was, thinking about people, about Daisy, in a way I'd never meant to.

Restless now, I rolled onto my back. Daisy was asleep, her chest rising and falling in deep, even breaths, her face softened in sleep. She was a brown-haired angel, and everything about her was so very lovely. With every fibre of my being I hated the fact that she'd seen me so weak, and worse—far worse—that she'd felt sorry for me.

Finally, sometime towards the pink-fingered dawn, sleep descended like a mist, and to my great relief the nightmare did not return.

Sunlight streaming from the floor-to-ceiling windows woke me slowly, bathing me in warmth. In the fog of sleep I was conscious of a warm body next to me, of a sleepy, feminine scent enveloping my senses. Still not even half awake, I reached for her and she came, melting into me with warm pliancy. My lips found hers as her arms wrapped around me, drawing me even closer.

I lost myself in her warmth, in the easy and open acceptance of her embrace, one knee sliding between her legs as I deepened the kiss, felt her yield beneath me. It was all so sleepily delicious, so wonderfully potent...the way her arms wound around me and her body arched against my questing hands. So easy...

Then consciousness sparked and I opened my eyes. Stared straight into hers, which were full of jarring compassion as well as heady desire. Then Daisy gave me a tender smile, a smile full of generosity and understanding, and it killed my lust at its very root.

In one abrupt movement I rolled off her, my stomach roiling even as my heart thudded, my body still sizzled with awareness and need.

'Matteo...'

Her voice was gentle—too gentle. I got out of bed, shrugging on a shirt and a pair of trousers, furious with both her and myself.

'What's wrong? Why did you...?'

'Stop? Because I don't need your pity, Daisy, especially in a moment like that one.' I gestured to the bed and she stayed silent, not denying it, which made it all so much worse. 'We leave for Paris within the hour,' I told her brusquely, and I walked out of the room without looking back.

Half an hour later, while I was immersed in work on my laptop—or at least trying to be—Daisy walked out of the bedroom, her hair damp from a shower, her expression composed and dignified, although I noted the wounded look in her eyes. Heaven spare me from a woman who wanted to save me.

'Are you ready?' I asked, keeping my voice brisk and businesslike. 'We should leave shortly.'

'Yes.'

She paused, looked as if she wanted to say something more, but I forestalled her by closing my laptop and rising. I was not interested in conversation—not any longer.

Although what I *was* interested in, I couldn't even say. Everything felt disordered and far more complicated than I'd ever expected or intended it to be. Making this marriage real was not nearly as simple as I'd hoped. In the depths of last night, when I'd lain awake, my mind seething over the possibilities and complications, I'd considered forgetting the whole thing. Just walking away. It would be infinitely easier. And yet...

I had never been a quitter, and the fact remained that I still needed an heir. I still wanted a wife. But it would have to be on my terms. Always.

And, I decided grimly, I knew just how to make that happen.

CHAPTER TEN

'*TRÈS BELLE, MADAME, très belle!*'

I smiled nervously at my unfamiliar reflection. For the last few days I'd been pampered, primped, and petted to within an inch of my life by a veritable army of stylists and beauticians. I didn't look anything like myself, but I supposed, considering the gala tonight, that was a good thing.

Since waking from his nightmare a few days ago Matteo had been intentionally remote, keeping conversation to a polite, brusque minimum. Strangely, I found I didn't mind. Once I would have let it hurt me. I would have assumed it meant he felt indifferent. But the experience of the last few days in his company had made me think, or at least hope, otherwise. It wasn't indifference; it was fear. Fear of being vulnerable, of being real—the kind of real he didn't want in our so-called 'real' marriage.

It had taken both careful thought and time for

me to conclude that Matteo didn't want compassion or understanding from me; they were anathema to him, and I almost understood that. Feeling vulnerable was hard enough—having someone know it and respond accordingly was even worse. So I didn't. I played by his rules and I kept to the game, meeting his courtesy with a careful composure of my own, although sometimes it felt like no more than a mask.

Was it even working? Was I doing the right thing? Trying to slip under his defences, win his trust and, yes, even his heart without him realising? Or was I just continuing to be the naïve and deluded greenhorn I'd been all along? Hoping for something better when nothing good was coming my way?

I took a deep breath and met my reflection full-on. This was the course I'd chosen and I was set on it…at least for the next two weeks. After that, who could say? I didn't want to think about what might or might not happen then.

A quick tapping sounded at the door. 'Are you ready?' Matteo called. 'We need to leave for the gala in fifteen minutes.'

I glanced back at the team of stylists and make-up artists who had turned this ugly duckling into an uncertain swan. 'Am I ready?'

'Mais oui, ma cherié!'

I smiled, nervousness making my heart skitter like a marble in a pinball machine, and then, taking a deep breath, I reached for my bag and headed out to the sitting room of our enormous penthouse suite in the heart of Paris, where Matteo was waiting for me.

I'd barely seen him these last few days; he'd been working and I'd been a lump of clay being pounded into sophisticated shape. We'd spent the nights together, however. Despite his nightmare, Matteo continued to sleep by my side. But he never even tried to touch me. I told myself I didn't mind, even as I ached.

Now I paused on the threshold of the room. His back was to me as he gazed out at Paris on a starry night, the Eiffel Tower a beacon of light in the distance.

'Matteo...' I said quietly.

Slowly he turned around. His pupils flared as he took me in from top to bottom—my hair in a loose chignon, with tendrils framing my face, my face expertly made up in a way the beautician had assured me was 'natural', my nails manicured and polished, my skin exfoliated and buffed and lotioned to a golden sheen. And, of course, the dress…

I'd tried on six dresses before Monique, my personal stylist, had insisted on this one—a shimmering column of topaz silk that flowed from one shoulder, nipped in at the waist, and then puddled in gold around my ankles.

Now I stood there, waiting for his verdict. 'Do I pass muster?' I asked as lightly as I could. I was terrified about what was ahead—hobnobbing with socialites and entrepreneurs, people who intimidated me without even trying.

'Pass muster?' Matteo came towards me, his hands outstretched to capture mine and draw me to him. 'You look stunning, *glykia mou*. You will be the most beautiful woman in the room.'

I laughed shakily. 'I think that might be spreading it a bit thick.'

'Not at all.'

Smiling, he brushed a kiss across my lips that felt like a promise—of what, exactly, my stomach fizzed at considering. For the last few days Matteo had kept his distance, both physically and emotionally, but with my hands in his and the touch of his lips making my own tingle I was beginning to have hope that was changing. That *he* was. That *we* were.

'Your outfit is perfect,' Matteo said, 'save for one thing.'

I looked down at my silk gown, eyebrows raised. 'And what is that?'

'This.'

From the pocket of his tuxedo he took a small black velvet box that made my heart judder.

'Matteo…'

'I should have given it to you before…at the beginning.' He opened the box to reveal two rings—one was a diamond flanked by two sapphires, the other a simple platinum band. Engagement and wedding rings. 'May I put them on you?'

Wordlessly, I nodded. It felt more sacred than the ceremony three years ago, having him slip on those rings. They were heavy on my hand, winking in the light.

'They're beautiful,' I whispered.

'And *you're* beautiful. But you need something just a little bit more.' With a smile, he took another black velvet box, this one long and slender, from his other pocket.

I let out an uncertain laugh. 'How many jewels have you pocketed?'

'Just this.' He opened the box for my inspection, and I drew a sharp breath at the diamond-encrusted topaz pendant that nestled amidst the ivory silk.

'It's beautiful.'

'Let me put it on you.'

I turned around for him to fasten the necklace. The stones were cool and heavy against my skin and his fingertips brushed the nape of my neck, each barely-there touch making me shiver.

Then, even more electrifying, I felt Matteo kiss the back of my neck, his warm lips lingering on my skin, his hands on my bare arms.

'You are so lovely, *glykia mou*. I look forward to tonight.'

I didn't think I was imagining the import in his words—something beyond mere innuendo. He wasn't thinking of the party, and neither was I. After days of barely any physical contact, and a more worrying emotional remoteness, my heart and my body both craved this intimacy. I was ready.

Paris was strewn with stars as we took a limousine to the party that was being held in a private ballroom at the Louvre. The night wrapped like dark velvet around us. Nerves jumped and writhed in my stomach—not just for the party and the intimidation factor of mingling with well-heeled guests, but being on Matteo's arm.

'I'm so nervous,' I admitted. 'What if everyone thinks I'm a country bumpkin?'

'They won't—and even if they do I don't give a toss about their opinion,' Matteo replied. 'They're nothing but pretenders and parasites. Bottom feeders.'

I drew back a little at his utterly dismissive tone. 'But they're the cream of society. And they're who you've socialised with all the time.'

He shrugged. 'Needs must.'

'You don't like *any* of them? Or respect them?'

I didn't know whether to feel sorry for the faceless mass he'd just dismissed or for the man who was so clearly alone. *Lonely.* More and more I was realising that Matteo's hard exterior hid a core of vulnerability, glimpses of which made me both ache and yearn—but I knew better than to show him that.

When Matteo saw my compassion, my care, he withdrew. Perhaps he wasn't used to it; perhaps he simply hated being vulnerable. Perhaps, unlike me, he wasn't longing for another person to connect with, to understand and, yes, to love.

But I was staking everything—my heart, my hope, my life—that he was. I just wasn't going to let him know. *Yet.* When I would feel brave enough—when he might want me to—I wasn't ready to consider. In the meantime I'd decided to gamble.

'I think,' Matteo told me curtly, 'it is more a matter of them not liking me. But that is utterly beside the point because I am completely indifferent to them.' He turned his head away to stare out of the window. 'We're almost there.'

I was determined to keep my emotional distance from Daisy, as I had been doing these last few days, and yet somehow she drew emotion from me, like siphoning off poison. *Why* had I spoken about the people at the party that way?

It was true enough: the women might want to warm my bed and the men might be awed by my wealth and power, but I was still the bastard child who hadn't been good enough until my grandfather had had no recourse but to accept me. Everyone knew it, even if they knew better than to speak of it.

Still, I hadn't meant to say as much to Daisy. I'd been so careful these last few days—keeping myself distant, trusting that the lack of physical contact would make her ache. It was certainly making *me* ache. I'd spent three sleepless nights staring gritty-eyed at the ceiling while Daisy lay curled up and sleeping just a scant few feet from me. Not reaching for her had taken all my self-control.

But tonight was going to be different. Tonight I was going to show Daisy to the world, stake my claim in public, and then stake it again in private. Tonight we would finally become man and wife, as we were always meant to be. And there was going to be nothing emotional about it.

The limo pulled up to the Louvre and a valet hurried to open the door, taking Daisy's hand to help her out. There was a scattering of paparazzi, as there always was at events like these, and flashbulbs began to pop as I emerged from the limo and took her hand.

'I wasn't expecting cameras…' Daisy murmured, her hand small and icy in mine.

'For the gossip tabloids,' I dismissed.

'They're all going to be wondering who I am…'

'They'll find out soon enough.'

'Wait…what?' She turned to me, her lovely eyes wide with surprise. 'What do you mean? You're not going to *tell* them…?'

'Why not?'

'Because this is a trial…'

She sounded uncertain, and I pounced on it.

'What would you rather, Daisy? I introduce you as my wife, or my latest mistress?'

Her chin tilted up a notch. 'I suppose there's no other option?'

'Of course not.'

'And will you tell them how long we've been married? That I've been tucked away like a dirty secret for three years while you've worked your way through who knows how many women?'

There was no spite in her voice, only bleak honesty.

'That is hardly how I would describe it, and in any case no one needs to know how long we've been married—just that we *are*.'

We were entering the museum, and she faltered at the archway. 'I'm going to be torn to pieces,' she whispered. 'Everyone's going to wonder what on earth you were thinking, marrying a nobody like me.'

'I assure you, no one will think any such thing.

I won't let them.' I spoke fiercely, more fiercely than I meant to, hating the thought of anyone looking down on her. 'Besides, it isn't true. You aren't a nobody, Daisy Dias. You are a beautiful, poised, accomplished businesswoman in your own right, and I'm proud and honoured to have you on my arm, as my wife.'

Tears sparkled like tiny diamonds on her lashes as she looked at me in amazement. 'Matteo…do you really mean that?'

With an uncomfortable jolt, I realised that I did. 'Yes, I do.'

I felt as if I were making more of a proclamation than I'd intended, but I reminded myself that I hadn't said anything about feelings. About caring.

'Now, let's get this party started,' I said with a smile, and I took a starched handkerchief from my pocket to dab carefully at her eyes. She gave me a tremulous smile in response.

'Thank you,' she whispered, and I didn't reply, because I'd surely said too much already.

It became apparent within just a few minutes of our arrival that Daisy had absolutely nothing to fear. She was luminous, and people were drawn to her inner beauty and natural warmth just as I was. Of course there were a few dagger-eyed darlings who unsheathed their claws, but Daisy simply ignored them.

I watched, with a glass of champagne raised to my lips, as she chatted to a billionaire's wife about—of all things—quilting. Apparently the woman had a hobby... Daisy moved her arms in elegant arcs as she explained, I supposed, how one went about making a quilt, and the woman—who was wearing over a million euros' worth of diamonds—listened in rapt attention. Who knew?

'Hello, Matteo.'

I started at the feel of an arm that was winding through mine, and looked down at the pair of cat-green eyes narrowed up at me. 'Hello, Veronique.' Just about the last person I wished to see, but I supposed it was inevitable.

'You haven't rung.' She pouted prettily—except it wasn't.

'Our liaison is over.' I disentangled my arm and took a step away from her. 'I thought I made that clear when we last saw each other.'

Only two weeks ago, but it felt like a lifetime. It *was* a lifetime.

'Because of...*that*?'

She nodded towards Daisy and my fingers tightened around the stem of my glass.

'That,' I informed her coldly, 'is my wife. And I'd thank you to speak of her with the highest respect.'

Veronique's face twisted in angry, ugly shock. 'You got *married*?'

'So it would seem.'

'In the last two weeks? I don't believe you.'

'Believe it.' I was tight-lipped, staring into the distance, wanting her gone.

'No, I don't think so. The way she marched into that ballroom, looking furious... You've been married for a while, haven't you? And now you've decided to trot her out like a show pony—heaven only knows why.'

I did not deign to reply, my jaw and fists both clenched.

Veronique let out a hard laugh. 'Some marriage,' she said, and walked off.

I cursed myself a thousand times for not handling that altercation better. I watched out of the corner of my eye as Veronique hurried towards a cluster of chatting women and whispered in one of their ears. The gossip was already spreading.

I joined Daisy, slipping an arm around her

waist to anchor her to me in the coming storm. She shot me a startled, pleased look, before resuming her discussion of stitching, or sewing, or whatever it was she was going on about. My mind was elsewhere as I watched the storm brew, one whisper at a time.

Instinctively my arm tightened around Daisy's waist and she glanced at me again, a wrinkle of worry marring her smooth forehead.

'Matteo…?'

'I'm just so fascinated by your knowledge,' I said with a smile. I glanced at her companion, my eyebrows raised. 'Did you know my wife runs her own textile company?'

'It's not quite as grand as that…' Daisy protested, and then they were off again, chatting away, while my stomach tightened with anxiety.

How would Daisy react to everyone knowing she'd been my secret? My tucked away and, as it turned out, not very convenient wife? Would it ruin all my plans?

'I'm just going to nip to the ladies',' Daisy said, and I watched, dread seeping into my stomach like acid, as a woman broke away from a gossipy cluster and headed towards the powder room as well—no doubt to interrogate Daisy or perhaps just skewer her with a few stiletto-sharp innuendoes.

Heaven help us both.

She was gone for fifteen excruciating minutes while I considered my options. Deny how the information had been leaked out? No. I was no coward, and I instinctively abhorred the idea of lying to Daisy. Make light of it, because I didn't care what any of these vapid, rabid social climbers thought? No, because I knew *she* would. Accept it and show the world that things were different now? *Yes.*

Even as part of me thrilled to the idea of making my marriage known in every aspect, another part quelled at the thought of people assuming we'd fallen in love with each other. Thinking I was weak...

Because it *was* weak to buy into that illusion. To be held hostage to your feelings. I knew that better than anyone, because I had once been such an unfortunate, misinformed prisoner.

Finally Daisy emerged from the ladies' room. I could tell just by looking at her that she'd heard. Her face was too composed, a touch resigned. Still, it could have been worse.

I started towards her. 'Daisy...'

'The cat is out of the bag.' Her smile was both wry and painful. 'I heard the gossip in the ladies'. I think they *wanted* me to hear.'

'Daisy, I'm sorry…'

'What do you have to be sorry for, Matteo?' Up went her chin in a stance I suspected Daisy had adopted for most of her life. 'It's the truth.'

She pressed her lips together, as if steeling herself, and I took hold of her arm, drawing her to me.

'What were those women saying?' I asked in a low voice.

'Oh, the expected. You had a wife tucked away but obviously didn't think much of her.'

'Daisy—'

'And the only reason you're trotting me out now is because I made a fuss at that ball a few weeks ago. Otherwise I'd still be firmly in the cupboard.'

'I'm sorry,' I said again, meaning it. I hated to see her hurt—especially by this vicious brood of pointless vipers.

'Like I said, you have nothing to be sorry for. It's the truth, isn't it? We wouldn't be here—*I* wouldn't be here—if I hadn't marched up to you at that stupid party.' She gave a hollow laugh. 'Goodness only knows what I was thinking.'

'I'm glad you did,' I told her—and it was something else I meant. Utterly.

'Are you? Because I can put up with anything anyone says if that's the truth. Things *are* different now, aren't they?'

She gazed up at me, her eyes sparkling the same jewelled shade as the pendant I'd put around her neck. And while part of me wanted to remind her...*not that different*...another part of me silenced the voice of reason completely.

'Of course they are.' I took both her slender hands in mine as I brushed a kiss across her lips for all and sundry to see. 'Of course they are,' I murmured against her lips.

She nodded, her eyes closed, her whole body accepting, and suddenly I couldn't bear to be in that stuffy ballroom for another second.

'Let's get out of here,' I said against her lips. 'Now.'

Daisy's eyes fluttered open and she gazed at me for a long moment, clearly understanding what I was really saying—and accepting it along with everything else.

'All right,' she whispered.

And then I was taking her by the hand, drawing her out to the night, and neither of us was looking back.

CHAPTER ELEVEN

EVERYTHING IN ME TINGLED—no, *sparkled*—as Matteo opened the door to the waiting limo himself. I knew what I'd agreed to and my heart sang even as my stomach tightened with nerves. Was I sure about this? Yes. Did I know what I was doing? Not remotely.

The vicious gossip I know I'd been meant to overhear had stung, but only briefly. Like Matteo, I realised I didn't care about the circling crows of society, only the people who were genuine, like the woman I'd met who had shown such an interest in quilting.

And Matteo. I cared about him. More and more. I couldn't deny it to myself even if I knew better than to whisper a word of it to him. Which was why I was here, speeding through the darkness with Matteo next to me, knowing what was ahead. Sort of.

The limo pulled up in front of Arides International, one of the dozens of luxury hotels in the group that Matteo was CEO of. A white-gloved valet opened the door, and Matteo murmured his thanks before drawing me out of the car and into the building.

My every sense felt heightened as we walked through the lobby, where the chandeliers suspended above us glittered with a fierce light, the tinkle of crystal and laughter a symphony of sound. And Matteo's hand was in mine…his fingers warm and dry and strong, drawing me ever forward.

Neither of us spoke in the lift as it soared up to the presidential penthouse where Matteo always stayed. He swiped the key card with one efficient movement and then tossed it onto a marble table in the hall before turning to me. My heart thudded so loudly I feared he could hear it—or see it, beneath the thin silk of my dress. I leaned against the closed door, breathless and expectant.

'Daisy.'

The way he said my name, a statement of both possession and intent, thrilled me to the core. He held out his hand and I took it, our fingers lacing together as he pulled me towards him.

Our hips bumped and heat flared but Matteo took his time, brushing his lips across mine once, twice, and then settling them there. I drank him in, every sense fizzing, as we kissed and kissed and it felt as if the whole world fell away. *I could be happy just like this, kissing him for ever*, I thought hazily, even as an insistent, molten part of me knew that I could not.

And Matteo knew it too, for he broke the kiss and started walking backwards towards the bedroom, a sleepy smile on his face, his fingers still laced with mine.

'No need to rush this,' he murmured as he pulled me along. And I went—willingly, *wantonly*, I went.

'No indeed,' I managed with a shaky laugh.

Already I was feeling out of my depth. Did Matteo know how little experience I had when it came to bedroom matters? He would certainly guess, but I wondered whether I should tell the truth of it to him now.

The bedroom was full of shadows and moonlight, the bed wide and inviting, a gold silk duvet piled high with embroidered pillows. Words were bottled up in my throat and then they sank towards my toes. I couldn't tell him. It would ruin the mood. I would feel ridiculous—even more gauche than I already did. And I was embarrassed enough already, just standing here with all my clothes on, while Matteo gazed at me, his eyes and his smile gleaming with admiration as well as something like avarice.

'You're so lovely, Daisy.'

He murmured the words, his hands spanning my waist as he kissed me again, his mouth slanting over mine with gentle yet persuasive possession.

'So, so lovely,' he whispered.

And then he kissed me again and I was lost.

I clutched at his shoulders, his back, anything I could get purchase on as his kiss consumed me. Then he stepped back and I was bereft, his absence a cold emptiness inside me.

With one finger he touched the pendant nestled in the hollow of my throat. 'We'll save that for last,' he said. 'Or maybe we'll keep it on.'

I didn't know what he meant until, in one sinuous and assured movement, he tugged the zip of my dress from its top to the small of my back. The dress fell away, pooling about my waist. Cool air puckered my skin and I fought the urge to cover myself, for I wasn't wearing a bra. I'd never been naked in front of another human being, and I felt it keenly now.

Matteo's gaze roved over me, a small smile curving his lips. 'You really are perfect, Daisy.'

'Hardly perfect.' I nodded towards his pristine tuxedo. 'What about you?'

'Ah, yes.' He arched an eyebrow in wicked challenge before spreading his arms wide. 'Shall you do the honours?'

I let out a little disbelieving laugh before I realised he was serious. Emboldened by the blatant look of desire in his eyes, I moved towards him and the dress slithered to my ankles. I stepped out of it, conscious that I was wearing nothing but a pair of high heels, scrappy silk knickers, and a necklace that cost a fortune. I would have felt absurd, except the expression on Matteo's face made me feel beautiful. Sexy. *Desired.*

Fumbling a little, I undid his bow tie and tossed it aside. Matteo watched me from under half-lowered lids, colour slashed on each cheekbone. As I moved down his shirt, my fingers clumsy on the studs, I felt the thud of his heart against my palm. He was affected—as affected as I was.

The cummerbund took some doing, and I laughed a little. 'I'm not very experienced at this.'

'That hardly matters. You're doing an excellent job,' he said huskily.

Finally the thing was off, and I tossed it aside with a shuddering breath. Using both my hands, I spread his shirt wide so I could take in the magnificence of his chest—tanned and perfectly sculpted. I outlined the ridges of his pectorals with my fingertips, amazed at how beautiful he was, and Matteo let out a ragged laugh.

'*Glykia mou*, what you do to me... No other woman has affected me like this.'

I glanced up at him, shocked. 'Is that really true?'

'It is.' He captured my hand with his own. 'But I do not want to talk or think of them—only of you.'

Then, in one elegant swoop, he caught me in his arms and laid me down on the bed. I kicked off my heels, watched as his eyes glinted silver and he undid his trousers, kicking them off with impatience, and then following with his shirt.

Then he lay down next to me, one arm braced over my head as he smiled down at me.

'I'm nervous,' I whispered.

'There is nothing to be nervous about, I promise you.'

He sealed that promise with a lingering kiss, and then he began to move lower, kissing my jaw, the curve of my neck, and then lifting the heavy pendant to press a kiss to the hollow of my throat. Each kiss made me shiver with longing and excitement, pleasure arcing through me at every brush of his lips.

Then his mouth moved even lower, and I squirmed with pleasure and shock as he kissed my breasts in turn, lavishing each with attention they had never known before.

'Matteo…' I half gasped his name as his mouth went lower yet, kissing his way down to my navel. No one had ever touched me like this. No one had ever made me feel like this.

Then his hand brushed between my legs, fingers seeking the damp heat that resided there, and I moaned aloud. The sound was one I'd never heard myself make before. Everything felt new and shockingly wonderful. His fingers were deft and knowing, touching me in a way that sent waves of pleasure spiralling through me, so intense I responded without even realising I was doing so—arching my hips, grabbing his hand.

'Easy, *glykia mou*.'

'You make me feel…' I gasped, not even sure what I was saying. But in any case I didn't need to say it.

'I know,' he said, and he kissed me again as his fingers continued to work their magic, and I felt a sense of urgency building inside me, as if I were climbing a spiral set of stairs, higher and higher, desperate to reach the top...

'Matteo!'

His name exploded from me as I convulsed under his touch, my body giving itself up to the dazzling wash of sensations that shuddered through me in a tide of pleasure. I'd never felt anything like it in my life, and I lay there, staring up at him with dazed eyes, boneless and spent.

'And that is just the beginning,' he said with a growl as he rolled on top of me.

'The beginning...' I felt as if everything in me had ended, and yet already a new, deeper need licked at me as Matteo held himself above me.

I braced myself for the invasion, tense even as I was ready—so ready.

Matteo began to slid inside, pausing as I winced just a little.

'Daisy...?'

'Sorry,' I muttered as I adjusted to the incredibly foreign feeling of him inside me. 'This is very...new.'

'New? Do you mean...?'

'Yes.' My voice came out in a suffocated whisper as I hid my blushing face against his shoulder. 'I didn't want to tell you.'

'Why ever not?' He gasped out the words, clearly using a superhuman level of restraint to keep himself from going any farther.

'I don't know. I thought it might put you off.'

'Put me off? *Glykia mou*, why would it do that? Do you know me at *all*?'

Yes, I thought as my body opened to accept his. *Yes, I do know you—better than you think... perhaps even more than you want. I know you, Matteo. I know you.*

And then I gave myself up to the feeling—and to him.

'Daisy...'

Her name was the only word on my lips, in my mind, as we spiralled towards that dizzying peak together. As she cried out softly, wrapping her legs around me, I had never expected to feel so much. Physical sensation, base pleasure—yes. I prided myself on giving that, as well as receiving it. But the feeling as Daisy surrendered herself to me, her body accepting and enfolding mine... As I looked down at her flushed face, her eyes dazed not just with passion but with something deeper, I realised that we were *joined*, truly as one in that moment. Man and wife.

Man and wife.

That blew me away. It left me shattered, physically replete and emotionally overwhelmed as I wrapped her in my arms, breathed in her scent, let her *envelop* me. I had never expected to experience such intensity—not mere pleasure, but emotion. Depth and need and *caring*.

I hated myself for it. This wasn't in the plan. This wasn't in the plan at all. And, worst of all, I knew Daisy felt it too—perhaps even felt it in me.

This was a disaster.

I rolled off her, my heart thudding in my chest as the aftershocks of our shared climax rippled through us both. We hadn't even used birth control—something I'd been intending to do, but had forgotten in the moment. I wondered if Daisy even realised.

She was silent, a faint smile on her lovely face, her hair tousled in a golden-brown cloud against the pillow. She still wore the pendant I'd given her and it gleamed against her golden skin. She looked like a painting—lush and ripe and so very beautiful.

I got out of bed.

'Matteo…?'

'I'm just going for a drink of water.' I tried not to speak brusquely because even now, when everything in me was both reeling and recoiling, I didn't want to hurt her—more fool me.

In the kitchenette of our suite I took a few deep, steadying breaths. I caught my reflection in the polished glass of a cupboard and saw how hollow-eyed I looked, as if someone had carved something right out of me. Perhaps they—*she*—had.

I took a long draught of water, stalling for time, trying to think how I should play this. My instinct was to go into chilly withdrawal—my usual reaction when I felt anyone was breaching my defences.

But no one had scaled the walls the way Daisy had; they were crumbling all around me. I couldn't retreat that way—not with her. It would be too cruel. It was a thought that made my mouth twitch in disbelief, because when had I ever cared about that? Yet somehow I did.

No, I decided, I would play it light. Easy. The

way I had fully intended this evening to be when I had planned it. Perhaps if I pretended long enough, it would really be the case. Daisy would believe me, and I'd even believe myself.

On impulse, I grabbed a bottle of champagne from the fridge, and two crystal flutes, and strolled back into the bedroom wearing nothing but a smile.

Daisy scooted up in bed, the sheet covering her breasts, her hair tucked behind her ears. She smiled at me uncertainly, and the hesitation I saw in her eyes made me ache in a way I didn't like.

'Champagne.' I brandished the bottle. 'To celebrate.'

'What are we celebrating, exactly?'

'Us.' I popped the cork on the champagne and poured two glasses to near overflowing. 'That was truly wonderful.'

Her smile remained filled with uncertainty. That wasn't quite the sweet nothing she'd been hoping to hear, but I pretended not to notice.

'Cheers, Daisy,' I said, and raised my glass.

After a second's pause she clinked her glass with mine and we both sipped.

'So…the Caribbean in a few days,' I said, my tone deliberately nonchalant. 'I can't wait to

show you the beaches. We'll go scuba diving…
have you ever been?'

She gave a disbelieving laugh. 'What do *you*
think?'

'At least you have a passport,' I said lightly. I'd
had it rushed through when we were first married.

She nodded slowly. 'Yes, I suppose.'

Her golden-brown gaze searched mine for a
moment, probing and testing me while I looked
blandly back. Whatever she was looking for she
didn't find, and she put her champagne aside and
got out of bed, reaching for a robe.

'Come back to bed.' The words burst from me
before I could think them through.

She gave me a fleeting smile. 'I will.'

It was foolish to feel bereft, to wonder what
she was thinking—and, worse, to *want* to know.
For nearly thirty-five years I'd prided myself on
not needing anyone, and more importantly, not
caring. At an early age I'd discovered love to be
the illusion it was—the *evil* illusion. Because no
matter how hard you tried to earn it, work for it,
it was never yours for the taking. And the reason for that was, I had decided a long time ago,
because it wasn't real in the first place.

I had Andreas to thank for teaching me that lesson—although of course he hadn't meant to. Andreas and my grandfather. Because I'd seen how my grandfather's love for my half-brother had turned to ash the moment he hadn't been useful any more. He'd banished him to the top floor of his house and never visited him at all. That had hurt almost as much as his complete rejection of *me*.

Seeing that change had made me realise just how pointless and arbitrary love was—how fleeting and foolish and *false*. And I was glad to have learned it when I was young. When I'd needed to.

With my mouth set in a grim line, I drained the rest of my champagne and then stretched out in bed, determined to relax.

Let Daisy sulk. Let her be sad. I wasn't going to chase after her—I wasn't going to chivvy her out of her melancholy mood like a child who needed to be given sweets.

But when she returned to bed twenty minutes later she surprised me, because she wasn't sulking at all. She smiled at me and then, with a hint of playfulness, shrugged off her robe.

My eyebrows rose. 'I could get used to this,' I said.

'So could I.'

Still smiling, she stretched out next to me and opened her arms, everything about her a warm invitation.

What could I do but take her in my own? The feeling of her body nestled close to mine was exquisite, and the kiss she gave me so freely was triumph. She was playing by my rules. She'd received, understood, and accepted them. I could feel it in the way she both responded and surrendered, and afterwards, both of us sated a second time, in the way she held out her champagne glass for a refill, a small smile playing about her mouth, her eyebrows slightly raised, as if to say, *See? I get it. I understand.*

I filled it gladly, trying not to notice the sadness that lingered in her eyes like a shadow in the corner of the room—and trying not to feel it myself, because that was ridiculous.

This was exactly what I wanted. It had to be.

CHAPTER TWELVE

'WELCOME TO ST CRISTIANO!'

I smiled as Matteo and I headed through the front archway of his newest luxury resort. A young woman, wearing the hotel staff uniform of white polo shirt and tan skirt, had stepped forward to hand me a bouquet of lilies and orchids in vivid pinks and purples.

'Thank you, they're beautiful,' I said, giving her a warm smile.

She smiled back and I glanced at Matteo, who was looking around the hotel in narrow-eyed assessment. It had been five days since we'd been at the gala in Paris—since we'd made our marriage oh-so-real. And it had continued to be very much *real* as we'd toured Paris, had dinner in several Michelin-starred restaurants, met his business associates and spent more time than I ever had before in bed, learning and loving each other's bodies. In addition, Matteo had showered me with more jewels and clothes than I knew what to do with.

I was overwhelmed by the elegance, indulgence, and the sheer decadent luxury of everything Matteo gave me so freely, seeming to take pleasure in my pleasure. He gave me everything—everything but himself. And I was trying to be happy with that. I was trying to let it be enough, for now, because I still had so much hope that things would change. The very fact that he was holding back meant there was something *to* hold back—a depth of emotion he wasn't yet ready to reveal. And I could wait; it had only been a few weeks, after all.

'This is amazing,' I murmured as the staff led us through an enormous lobby filled with tropical flowers and tinkling fountains. Latticed shutters were thrown open to the hotel's inner courtyard, with a set of five cascading pools.

'It should be,' Matteo returned. 'It's one of my most luxurious hotels. Everything must be top drawer.'

He snapped his fingers and a bellboy came hurrying over.

'Sir?'

'Please take our luggage to the Amaryllis Bungalow.'

'Very good, sir.'

'We're not staying in the presidential suite this time?' I teased.

Matteo smiled and shook his head. 'Even better.'

We walked through the lobby and then outside, along a strip of soft, white sand beach, to a bungalow in its own verdant garden.

'These are better than suites,' Matteo announced as he ushered me into the bungalow's sumptuous living area, its French windows open to the beach, the sea only a few metres away. 'Complete privacy,' he added as he pulled me towards him.

The luggage had already been delivered, and the bellboy had withdrawn with discreet haste. I tilted my head up for Matteo's kiss, revelling in the way he made me feel. It was as if I came alive in his arms. I didn't think I would ever grow tired of it.

'Let me give you the full tour,' Matteo murmured as he steered me towards the back of the bungalow. 'Starting with the bedroom.'

Within minutes he'd stripped me of the cotton

sundress I'd worn for travel, and shucked off his linen business suit in a few quick movements. Naked, we tangled on the sheets, the *shooshing* sound of the sea the perfect background symphony to our lovemaking.

And it *was* lovemaking—at least for me. I still believed Matteo felt something too—something more than he was willing to admit. That first night when he'd left our bed so quickly it had been hard not to feel scorned and wounded. But I hadn't; I'd made myself accept his terms, because that was so clearly what they were.

This and no more.

But to that I added my own silent caveat—*for now.*

'How about some fruit punch?' Matteo asked lazily as he strolled from the bed towards the kitchen.

I watched him go, amazed at his self-confidence, his perfect physique, all lean, sinewy muscle, power and grace.

He returned with a platter of tropical fruit, a pitcher of punch and a couple of glasses.

'You're spoiling me,' I said, which had been my refrain for the last few days.

'I like spoiling you.' Matteo poured us both

drinks and handed me one. 'And you deserve to be spoiled. You haven't had enough spoiling in your life, as far as I'm concerned.'

I smiled and took a sip, nearly spluttering in surprise.

'Rum,' Matteo answered my silent question. 'It packs quite a kick.'

I laughed and took another sip. 'It certainly does.'

I wished we could spend the afternoon lazing in bed or by our private pool, but after a short while Matteo rose from the bed to dress, as I'd known he would.

'Duty calls,' he said with a grimace, and it heartened me that he would clearly rather stay with me than go to work.

That meant something, surely? Or was I being naïvely hopeful, even absurdly delusional, as I'd once been before? In unguarded moments, that was the fear that crept in and crouched in the corners of my heart. That Matteo wasn't going to change. That he couldn't.

'Take advantage of everything,' he said as he pulled on a freshly starched shirt. 'The pool, the beach… Tomas is our personal butler. All you have to do is press the intercom in the living area and he'll be here in a few minutes, if not sooner, to see to your every need.'

'I thought that was *your* job,' I dared to tease, and Matteo flashed a wicked smile.

'Indeed,' he said, dropping a lingering kiss on my lips. 'But he'll fetch your drinks.' He reached for his tie. 'We'll dine in the hotel's restaurant tonight, and the opening ball is tomorrow night—don't forget.'

'How could I?' Even though I'd been to a handful of such events over the last few days, they still made me nervous. I still felt like a country bumpkin inside. But Matteo had assured me that was no bad thing.

'People take to you,' he'd said. 'Your natural warmth, your down-to-earth personality…it's refreshing, *glykia mou*. Don't ever change.'

I reminded myself of that as I unpacked my clothes—far too many for only a weekend in the Caribbean, but Matteo was insistent that I should be completely kitted out. I had several evening gowns to choose from, both for this evening and tomorrow night, and with a smile I wondered which one I should surprise Matteo with tonight. Already my mind jumped ahead to the end of the evening, when he would peel it off me…

Banishing such thoughts for now, I checked in with Maria, to make sure Amanos Textiles was surviving without me, which it was, before heading to the pool to sunbathe and read the latest bestseller I'd picked up at the airport.

In the late afternoon, as the sun started to sink towards the aquamarine horizon, I decided to start getting ready for dinner.

The bungalow's bathroom was almost as large as its bedroom, with a huge marble tub and a double glass-walled shower. As I stood beneath the spray I marvelled yet again at my luxurious surroundings, as well as at the fact that I was with Matteo at all—*married* to him. Never mind my middle-of-the-night doubts; this was happiness, and my heart was full of it.

I started to sing—something I hadn't done in years, since Chris Dawson had told me the truth about my voice.

I'd always loved singing as a child; my grandmother had taught me hymns and folk songs, and I'd whiled away the many hours of scrubbing and cleaning with songs. I'd sung at church, as well, and had always been told my voice was lovely—a gift from God. Which was what had led to my disastrous attempt to make it as a singer in the big city.

Since Chris Dawson's crushing set-down, I hadn't sung at all, barely hummed under my breath. It was as if he'd killed something inside me. But today, when I was filled with joy, it came to life again.

'Daisy!'

Matteo's shocked voice had me whirling around in the shower and nearly slipping on the slick tiles.

'I didn't see you there.' I turned off the shower and reached for a robe, embarrassed that he'd caught me belting out a hymn. 'Sorry, I must have sounded like a frog.'

'Far from it.'

He was eyeing me oddly as I belted my robe and twisted a towel around my wet hair.

'You have a beautiful singing voice, Daisy.'

'Oh, *please*.' I made a face. 'Don't worry, Matteo, I was disabused of that notion a long time ago—as I believe I told you. I'm not entertaining dreams of being a famous singer any more, trust me. You don't have to humour me.'

He folded his arms. 'I'm not humouring you. You have a beautiful voice. Husky and sensual.'

I blushed and then shook my head, still refusing to believe his flattery. 'Really, you don't…'

'Daisy, when have I humoured *anybody*? I'm telling you the truth.' He frowned, his forehead scoring briefly with worry lines. 'Why don't you believe me?'

I hesitated, unwilling to delve into my rather desperate and sordid past. 'Someone told me the truth once,' I finally said. 'That's all.'

'And who was that?'

'One of New York's premier casting agents, so…' I walked past him into the bedroom, pulling the towel from my hair. 'I think he probably knows a bit more than you do about what a good voice sounds like.'

'A casting agent?' Matteo propped one shoulder against the door frame as he watched me riffle through my clothes. 'How did you end up singing in front of him?'

I shrugged, my eyes on the hangers in front of me. 'Lucky, I suppose.' *Or not.*

'Why, *glykia mou*, do I feel as if you're not telling me something?'

In two swift strides Matteo had crossed the room to me, stilling my pointless riffling of the clothes I couldn't think of wearing in this moment.

I glanced up at him warily. 'Why do you care so much, Matteo? It's old history.'

'It concerns you, and therefore it concerns me.'

It was an admission that should have thrilled me, but I was too reluctant to share this humiliating piece of my history to savour it. 'It's not important.'

'I think it is.'

'I'm sure you have things *you'd* rather not share,' I shot back, even though I suspected it was unwise. 'Do we have to tell each other everything?'

Matteo glowered at me. 'We are husband and wife, Daisy—'

'This is still just a trial.'

As soon as I said the words I wished I hadn't. Why on earth was I picking a fight? I didn't want to remind Matteo of the stupid trial; I didn't want to be angry with him or him with me. But neither did I want to tell him how naïve and stupid I was—how *used*.

Matteo's brows snapped together and his eyes blazed. Too late. He was angry.

'Is that how you still see it, Daisy?' he asked,

his voice a low growl. 'Truly?' He gestured to my middle. 'Do you realise we might have already created a baby together? I did not use protection that first time. Have you thought of that?'

Yes, I had—although I'd been too shy and nervous to mention it to him. Part of me half hoped I was pregnant. I knew it was probably unlikely but, dreamy fool that I was, I insisted on painting rainbows in a stormy sky.

'It has crossed my mind,' I admitted.

Matteo shook his head. 'Yet still you talk about a *trial*?' he demanded.

'I'm sorry,' I whispered. 'I didn't mean it. But why can't you just drop it, Matteo?' To my mortification, tears came to my eyes. 'It doesn't matter any more.'

'Clearly it still grieves you, and therefore it does matter.' Gently he wiped a tear that had trickled onto my cheek. 'Why can't you tell me, Daisy?'

'I… I don't know. It's embarrassing, I suppose, and it makes me feel about two feet tall.'

I sighed and pulled my robe more tightly around me as I succumbed to the inevitable. Embraced it. How could I expect Matteo to be more vulnerable, more open, if I wasn't willing to be so myself?

'I'll tell you, Matteo, if you really want to know.'

The sight of Daisy's tear-filled eyes, her slumped shoulders, filled me with something close to fury. Whatever memory she was holding close it was an incredibly painful one, and I hated that. I hated that far more than I should.

'I do want to know,' I said, taking her by the hand. 'But, more than that, I want you to *want* to tell me.'

'There's nothing you can do about it—'

'We shall see about that.'

Whoever had hurt my wife would pay. In some way, he'd pay.

'Come and sit down,' I urged, and with a surrendering sort of nod Daisy allowed me to lead her to one of the sofas in the living room. The sun was setting and the whole world was bathed in vivid orange and pink; the light gilded her with gold as she curled up in a corner of the sofa.

'I don't know where to begin,' she said, with a shaky, uncertain laugh.

'Begin at the beginning,' I told her as I tucked a damp tendril of hair behind her ear, because I felt the need to reassure her with my touch. 'Or wherever you feel you want to.'

'The beginning, I suppose, is back in Briar Valley.' She sighed and wrapped her arms around her knees. 'I always loved singing as a child, and Briar Valley is such a small place... I suppose I must have *some* talent, right?'

I opened my mouth to insist she had a great deal of talent, but she forestalled me with a shake of her head.

'Anyway, that's not the point. The point is, after my grandmother died I was at a loose end, to put it mildly. There was no money, and I didn't have many friends—most people my age had left Briar Valley long before I did. So I decided to hitch my wagon to the proverbial star and head to the city in search of fame and fortune.'

She had told me as much before, but there was a darker undercurrent to her words now.

'You wouldn't be the first person to do so, Daisy,' I said in a low voice.

I imagined her alone in the city, trying to make her way, innocent and optimistic, and my hackles rose in defence. Who had snuffed out her dreams—perhaps even worse?

'No, and I don't suppose I'll be the last. Anyway, I went to New York full of dreams and determination, and I believed that would be enough. Turns out you need talent too.'

'You *do* have talent,' I insisted.

Her voice in the shower had been amazing—husky and sensual and full of emotion. It angered me that she couldn't see it, that someone had kept her from believing in herself.

'Well, anyway...' Daisy resumed with a sad attempt at a smile. 'A casting agent saw me at an open audition and invited me for a private interview. I thought I was so lucky.'

Everything in me tensed as I sat up straight, staring at her fiercely. 'What are you saying, Daisy?'

Her lips trembled and she looked away. 'I'm sure you can guess.'

I could—and I very much didn't want to. My fists clenched instinctively and my heart raced. 'Did he...? Did he...?'

'He didn't get that far,' she assured me shakily. 'But far enough. Farther than I'd ever... I'd never even been kissed before that. And I wasn't again after...until you.'

That kiss in the ballroom, when I'd been so

ruthlessly trying to prove a point. Shame boiled through me; no wonder she had pushed me away.

'So what happened?' I asked in a low voice. 'What…what did he do to you?'

'As soon as I got into the room he…he made it clear.' She shook her head, the memory clearly painful. 'He said if I was nice to him he would be nice to me. Even then I wasn't sure what he meant! I was so naïve.'

'Innocent,' I ground out. 'You were innocent.'

'When I looked clueless he made it abundantly clear. He grabbed me and wrestled me onto the sofa…' She dabbed at her eyes. 'Well, you can imagine the rest. I got away before he…before he took things too far. But they went farther than I wanted.' She let out a shuddering breath. 'I was so stupid, Matteo. I told another waitress what had happened and she laughed at me, asked if I'd never heard of the casting couch. I really had no idea, but I should have—'

'There's no "should" in a situation like that, Daisy.' I cut her off with swift finality. 'The only "should" is that monster of a man should never have touched you.'

And when I found out who he was I'd make him regret it. Dearly.

'Still…' Daisy's smile wobbled and then slid off her face. 'I felt so guilty afterwards. I still do—which is part of why I didn't want to tell you.'

'Guilty?' I was horrified, and I had to take her in my arms. She snuggled against me, her cheek pressed to my chest. 'Why should you feel guilty?'

'Because I should have known. Because I should have made it clear why I was there. Because there were a few seconds when I didn't push him away. I was too shocked, I didn't know what to do, but because of that he might have got the wrong idea—'

'*No.* No, Daisy.' Gently I stroked her hair. 'This wasn't your fault and you shouldn't feel guilty— ever—about what happened. I know those are just words, and they can't necessarily change the way you feel or think, but they're true and necessary and I'll keep saying them until you believe them.'

Daisy let out a shuddering breath. 'Thank you, Matteo.'

As I sat and stroked her hair a realisation crept up on me—unfortunate, unwelcome and impossible to ignore. I wasn't much better than the creep who'd thrown her onto the casting couch. I'd manipulated her through our physical relationship, at least at the start and maybe even after. I'd insisted she share my bed, even if I didn't touch her while she was in it. Considering what Daisy had just told me, all those things that I had so easily justified to myself took on a sordid taint.

'Daisy,' I said in a low voice, 'if anything I've ever done…if you've ever felt…' I could barely say the words; they were bottled up in my throat.

Daisy twisted in my arms to look up at me, resting one hand against my cheek. 'Don't even say it, Matteo,' she protested gently. 'It was never that way between us.'

'But I—'

'Hush.' She kissed me on the lips, her breath whispering into mine. 'I'm crazy for you—don't you know that?'

Crazy for me.

I'd wanted to keep my distance, and for Daisy to keep hers. I'd done my best to make sure our relationship stayed purely physical. But in that moment I knew we'd crossed a line. We'd crossed it days ago, if only I'd had the sense, as well as the courage, to see it.

Because I was more than crazy for her. I was falling in love with her—and it absolutely terrified me.

CHAPTER THIRTEEN

'So you're Matteo's latest.'

The bored drawl, nearing a sneer, had me freezing in my four-inch gold stilettos. It was the night of the hotel's opening ball, and I'd just left Matteo to go and powder my nose in the ladies'.

Slowly I turned around to face my accuser—a louche-looking man in his forties, with one hand stuck in his trouser pocket as he surveyed me with thorough insolence.

'Excuse me?' I said, my voice as icy as I could make it. I lifted my chin to face him down, even though the lewd look on his face made my insides shrivel.

'You're Dias's latest. His whore.'

I jerked back as if I'd been slapped. I felt as if I'd been assaulted. Who *was* this man, and why was he treating me this way?

'I'm his wife,' I said, with as much cold disdain as I could muster. 'Now if you'll excuse me…'

I started to shoulder past him, but he grabbed my arm. Everything in me froze.

'Do you know who he is?' the man asked in a low, vicious voice. 'Do you know where he's come from?'

I stared at him in confusion, drawn despite myself and in spite of all I knew this man had to be. 'Where he's *come* from?'

'The gutter, darling. The absolute gutter. His mother was a Portuguese prostitute who dropped him on a doorstep. His poor grandfather had no choice but to take him in—although I'm sure he's regretted it every day since.'

'What?' I goggled at him, forgetting for a second that he was holding my arm, his body pressed alarmingly close to mine. 'What are you talking about?'

'Has he not told you?' the man mocked. 'He does like to keep his secrets. Likes to lord it over everyone, acting as if he's the *crème de la crème*, but everyone knows the truth. It's just that he's so wealthy…no one is willing to say it to his face.'

'But *you* are, obviously,' I said coldly, trying to jerk my arm out of his grasp.

The man held on, his nails starting to dig in. 'I am, and I'm doing you a favour by telling you.

Get out while you can. Take him for all he's worth while you're at it.'

'You're despicable.'

Again I tried to pull away, but the man just held on to me more tightly. True fear began to lick cold flames right through me. The crowded ballroom was only a few metres away, but we were alone in a narrow, darkened corridor. Anything could happen. Anything *might*.

For a few torturous seconds I was back in New York, struggling on that sofa, feeling hands and a mouth on me... My vision blurred and my stomach heaved as the man moved closer. I just stood there—waiting, frozen.

'Get your hands off her.'

Matteo's voice was low and deadly, and after an endless, awful pause the man finally released me.

I stumbled away from him with a gasp. 'Matteo...'

'She was begging for it, Dias,' the man drawled. 'Can't you tell? She wanted someone with *real* class.'

'Get out.' Seemingly from nowhere, two burly security guards materialised, each one grabbing the man by an arm and hustling him away.

I drew a shuddering breath, one hand pressed to my heart. Matteo looked at me—a hard, unyielding look, his eyes as cold and dark as gunmetal.

'Is it true?' he asked, in a low voice that throbbed with fury.

'What?' I gaped at him, his words piercing me like the sharpest dagger. 'You mean, what he said...? Are you *serious*?'

Matteo stared at me for another long moment, his jaw tight and bunched. 'Just answer the question. Did you welcome his attentions?'

I shook my head, my stomach roiling at his words. 'I can't believe you'd even ask me a question like that.'

'You're not answering it—'

'Because I won't stoop to such a horrible level!' I stared at him in disbelief and hurt. 'Matteo, why are you like this? After everything I told you yesterday, how can you ask me that?'

He stared at me for another hard moment. 'I'm sorry.' The words were gritted out. 'Let's just leave it.'

And then he turned on his heel and did just that, leaving me alone in the hallway, reeling from everything that had happened with the stranger—and with Matteo.

After a few stunned and awful moments I went into the ladies' and splashed water on my face. In the mirror my face was pale, my eyes wide and dazed. I still couldn't process everything that had happened—from the odious stranger's sneers about Matteo to his over-the-top, unprecedented response.

What had happened? What was going on?

With a shuddering breath I turned from my shocked reflection to head back to the party— mainly because I didn't know where else to go.

It was in full swing, with everyone chatting, laughing and swilling champagne as I slipped through the crowds, instinctively looking for Matteo. I still couldn't believe he'd just *left* me there. Why was he so angry with me? Did he actually think I'd invited that awful man's attentions?

My stomach cramped and tears stung my eyes. I couldn't believe how quickly everything had unravelled—especially since the last two days had been the sweetest we'd shared yet.

After telling Matteo about my awful experience with Chris Dawson he'd been so tender and caring. It had made my heart melt and my hope sing—because what else could this be but love? Or at least something close to it…something that was growing into it. Something I could start to trust.

We'd had a lovely leisurely dinner in a private room at the restaurant, and then strolled through the gardens in the moonlight, hand in hand, while Matteo had told me how he'd taken his grandfather's faltering empire and turned it into the global success it was today, dominating the luxury hotel market even as he refused to take the man's name, insisting on keeping his mother's.

Such a contrary tangle of emotions, and I'd wondered if he saw it in himself. As much as he hated his grandfather, part of him craved something from him—perhaps even love. And it had made me more determined to show him my love, even if he persisted in believing he didn't want it.

Back at the bungalow we'd made love tenderly, our bodies and hearts so in sync we'd needed no words as we moved and clung together.

Yes, this was love. At least it was on my part. I knew that now, and accepted it. I'd fallen in love with my husband. And I had started to hope, just a little, that he had fallen in love with me… whether he was willing to admit it to himself or not.

Today Matteo had worked all morning, and then we'd spent the afternoon lounging and laughing by the pool before getting ready for the party tonight. He'd been attentive and at my side for the entire event, save for my brief foray to the ladies', and now it felt as if everything had exploded.

Shaking my head, knowing I was in no mood for the party, I slipped through one of the many sets of French windows that led to the cascading pools, the water silver in the moonlight, the path down the bougainvillea-covered hillside lit by flickering tiki torches.

I walked past clusters of people, heedless of their speculative glances—everyone knew I was Matteo's wife, and they'd accepted it with varying degrees of surprise, pleasure or scepticism. I didn't care about any of them now; I only cared about Matteo and I didn't even know where he was.

I made my way down the hillside, past the pools, not even caring where I was going. I just wanted to get away—from the crowds, from my own clamouring thoughts.

At the bottom of the five pools the terrace was thankfully empty, and I leaned against the stone balustrade that overlooked the sea, listening to the comforting *whoosh* of the tide. The cool evening breeze blew the last of the tears from my eyes as I struggled to make sense of what had happened and figure out how to go on from here.

My confidence had taken an almighty knock, with Matteo turning on me so suddenly. It had brought all my old insecurities and fears to the fore, making me wonder if I really was delusional after all, in hoping that this was going to turn into something real. A *real* marriage…one with affection and respect and *love*.

Was I a fool for believing that? For thinking it could happen? Would it be better—smarter, safer—to cut my losses and go back to Amanos and the cold convenience of our former marriage?

Our supposed trial of two weeks was up in just a few days but, as Matteo had reminded me, I might already be pregnant. And what if I was overreacting to what might be a silly argument, the kind any couple had?

But in my heart I knew I wasn't. I knew there was something dark and hidden in Matteo, something he didn't want me to see. For a second I had seen it, and I was afraid that it changed everything. Or maybe it didn't. Maybe this was the reality I'd been blind to all along.

'Daisy.'

I stilled at the sound of his voice, everything in me aching. With my hands curled around the balustrade, my face towards the sea, I steeled myself for whatever happened next.

'What is it, Matteo?'

She looked like a sorrowful mermaid, gazing longingly out at the sea. Wisps of hair escaped the chignon one of the hotel's beauticians had styled for her earlier in the evening, and the sea-foam-green dress, its gauzy material embroidered with gold thread, blew about her legs, emphasising her slender, almost ethereal figure. She was lovely, and she was hurting, and it was my fault.

'I'm sorry,' I said simply.

I had no other words. I knew I never should have asked her if she'd welcomed that slug Farraday's attentions; it had been painfully and glaringly obvious that she had not. Of *course* she had not. And I'd known for years that Farraday hated me—not for the circumstances of my birth, but for my business success. He'd bid for this resort development on St Cristiano and I'd won it.

Daisy shook her head, her gaze still on the sea. 'Why?' she whispered.

I didn't pretend not to understand her. 'I don't know. I was angry…caught up in the moment. I am truly sorry.'

Slowly she turned, her face drawn in lines of sadness. 'I feel as if there are things you aren't telling me, Matteo. That you don't want to tell me.'

'What did Farraday say to you?'

'Is that his name? The man who—'

Jaw tight, I nodded. She stared at me for a long moment, her gaze moving over me slowly, as if she were trying to figure me out. To understand me, when I both hated and yet longed to be understood.

'He told me you were illegitimate,' she said at last. 'He said your mother was a prostitute who left you on your grandfather's doorstep.'

I nodded, accepting. Of course I'd never expected to hide the truth from her for ever. Too many people suspected or outright knew the truth, because when I was young my grandfather had not sought to hide it. It was only later that he regretted his show of bitterness.

'That doesn't matter to me,' Daisy said. 'I hope you know that, Matteo? The circumstances of your birth…' She shrugged. 'I'm illegitimate as well. My parents were never married.'

Surprise flickered through me. 'I didn't know that.'

'It didn't seem important.' She eyed me carefully. 'But this is? To you?'

Now I was the one to shrug. 'It matters little to me what side of the blanket you or I were born on, but unfortunately it mattered very much to my grandfather.'

Bitterness corroded my insides and felt like acid coating my throat. As much as I steeled myself not to care, I knew I did. I always had, and that was the awful, shaming truth of it. *Which was why I was trying so hard not to care about Daisy.* Not to let myself be vulnerable. Not to get hurt.

'Will you tell me?' Daisy asked softly. 'Please?'

Her voice was a tempting whisper, the siren

song of surrender, and part of me wanted to tell
her—fool that I was.

'You've heard most of it already,' I said.

'I feel as if I've only heard the beginning.'

Slowly she walked from the balustrade to the
side of the pool, pulling her dress up to reveal
slender calves and trim ankles. She stepped out
of her heels before sitting down at the side of
the pool, dipping her feet in the moonlit water,
and then she held out an arm, gesturing for me
to join her there.

After a long, lonely moment, I did.

I took off my shoes and socks, tossing them
aside before rolling up my trousers and dipping
my feet into the cool water alongside her. We
sat in a silence both companionable and strange
for a few minutes, the only sound the gentle tinkling of the water cascading down from the pool
above.

Daisy didn't push me—didn't say anything or
even raise her eyebrows in expectation. She just
waited, as if she could wait for ever.

'It's not quite true,' I finally said. 'My mother
wasn't a prostitute, as far as I know. But she was
poor, and she slept with my father to better herself. Unfortunately that didn't work out.'

'I'm sorry.'

'She left me on my grandfather's doorstep because she thought he would be able to provide a better life for me, and I suppose he has. My father died before I was born—a speedboat accident. He was drunk. His wife—he was married when he had an affair with my mother—insisted my grandfather take me in. She was living with him, but she was very frail, both emotionally and physically. She was also pregnant with my half-brother, Andreas.'

'That sounds…complicated.'

'In the end my grandfather made it very simple.' I could not keep the decades-old bitterness from spiking the words. 'My stepmother—if I can even call her that—died when Andreas and I were a year old. I don't remember her, but I know she tried to be kind. After that my grandfather took the gloves off.'

I swallowed hard, staring down at the water.

'What do you mean?' Daisy asked softly.

'He hated me. Despised and resented me as the bastard grandson—the one who didn't deserve anything, who reminded him of the son he'd hated for being a playboy and profligate. Because apparently I looked like my father, while Andreas looked like his mother. I think my grandfather would have thrown me out—left me at a convent, whatever—but for the stain it would have been on his reputation. Sometimes I wish he had.'

I shook my head as the dark tide of memories lapped at me, threatening to take over.

'Instead he made my life a misery.'

I thought of Eleni, the nanny who had showered Andreas with affection and me with scorn and hate. *You'll always be a bastard.* The locked cupboard… But I didn't want to go into those horrible and shaming details, so I just shrugged and explained the minimum.

'He let me know at every opportunity that he didn't want me there, and that I would never get a penny from him. Andreas was groomed as the heir and given every opportunity—private school, horse riding lessons, whatever… I was raised separately with a nanny, in a poorer neighbourhood. I learned how to fight at the local school.'

Where I'd been bullied mercilessly for being the posh boy, even though I was anything but.

'I was kept apart from them, and when my

grandfather did deign to see me I was ignored or insulted.'

Or worse. But again I kept silent. The last thing I wanted was Daisy's pity.

'It was a tough way to grow up,' I resumed, keeping my voice brisk. 'But in some ways it made me stronger, so I have my grandfather to thank for that.'

'But he made you the heir to his business...' Daisy said, her forehead furrowed with confusion. 'And he required you to marry... How does that fit in?'

My chest felt tight as memories washed over me. 'When we were thirteen, as I told you before, Andreas was in a skiing accident. He suffered a traumatic brain injury which left him in the mental state of an eight-year-old. He was no longer fit to take over the business, but I was. My grandfather hated that, let me tell you.'

'So he made your life even *more* of a misery?' Daisy surmised. 'Even though he needed you?'

'Something like that.'

There was a sudden transfer to boarding school, where I had the wrong accent, the wrong everything. Where the truth about me had always seemed to seep out like poison: *He's a bas-*

tard. His mother was a whore. And, worse, there were holidays back home, when my grandfather did his best to ignore me—or rage at me. At least Eleni was out of the picture by then…

'There's no love lost between us, as I told you three years ago.'

'So why did he require you to marry?'

I shrugged. 'Sheer perversity, perhaps? Or he might have hoped it would lend me respectability when he handed over the reins—which he knew he had to. He had cancer, and I'd already shown myself to be more than capable.'

'And then you married a down-and-out waitress instead of the blue blood I'm sure he was hoping for.' She shook her head. 'He must have loved that.'

'He was annoyed, yes.' I glanced at her. 'But the last thing I wanted was some snobby socialite.'

'So you chose me on purpose because of my lack of suitability?'

She sounded amused, but I still felt the need to be careful.

'Yes, I suppose… But you were suitable to me.'

'I don't mind, Matteo. I've never had pretensions to grandeur.'

'Which is one of the things I lo—like about you.' Horrified, I realised what word had been about to slip out of my mouth. 'But my grandfather doesn't matter to us, Daisy. You never even need to see him. I hope that you don't.'

'I think he *does* matter,' she returned sadly. 'He's obviously shaped who you are, whether you wanted him to or not. Is he still involved in the business?'

'Only as a figurehead. When I married I gained the controlling shares, and I will keep them for as long as I stay married—which I intend to. So he really doesn't concern us at all.' I reached for her hand, lacing her fingers through mine. 'And now you know.'

'Do I?'

She searched my face, clearly guessing there were things I hadn't said.

'You know enough.' I leaned over to brush my lips against hers. 'I really am sorry for being a jackass before,' I whispered against her mouth.

'Your apologies are so charming.' She smiled at me and I deepened the kiss, need flooding through me sweeter than ever before. I couldn't get enough of her—now or ever.

'Matteo…' Her voice became a mewl of urgency as she grabbed my shoulders, pulling me closer. We fell back on the terrace, barely aware of the hard stones beneath us as my hand slipped under her dress.

Lost in the daze of our shared passion, neither of us heard the quick footsteps, or even the clearing of a throat until it was too late.

'Mr Dias… I am so sorry to interrupt…'

I raised my head, infuriated that a member of staff should accost me in this way. Daisy scooted up to a sitting position, her face flaming as she adjusted her dress.

I straightened my tie, glowering at the young man. 'It had better be for good reason.'

'It is your grandfather, sir. He has just sent a telegram to the hotel. He requires your presence in Athens immediately.'

CHAPTER FOURTEEN

I GAZED BLINDLY out at the city streets as the limo slid through Athens' notoriously busy traffic. Next to me Matteo was glowering at his phone as he scrolled through emails, his jaw tight, his expression inscrutable.

Everything had changed since last night, when Matteo had received his grandfather's telegram.

'What does the old bastard want now?' he'd drawled as he'd glanced at the scant few lines. 'Just to see if I'll still come running when he crooks his finger, no doubt.'

'Perhaps it really is urgent,' I'd suggested tentatively. I felt as if I were swimming in deep water, having no idea of the emotional currents that swirled around us.

'Of course it's urgent,' Matteo had said scornfully. 'It always is with him. He's assembled the board—I have no choice but to go.'

'Do you have to do what the board says?'

'I have controlling shares, but if it's something

to do with the business I need to know. We're done here, anyway.'

He'd walked away from me without looking back, and I hadn't been able to help but wonder if his words were a portent—not for the business, but for us.

We're done here.

But things had felt as if they were just *beginning.*

And yet since that wretched telegram arrived Matteo had completely withdrawn from me, barely offering me two terse words together. I understood that he was focused on his grandfather and his business, but our relationship felt too new and fragile to be treated like this and survive.

Perhaps he wasn't intending it to.

All the old doubts plagued me as they had before—despite all we'd shared, all Matteo had shared. I'd finally felt as if he were being honest and vulnerable with me, and when he'd told me his grandfather didn't matter I'd chosen to believe him. How ill-timed that only a few minutes later his words were shown to be a lie.

How much else was a lie? How much of this real marriage was real at all?

Despair lapped at me like cold, dark water as I gazed blindly outside. I had no idea what was going to happen next.

'Where does your grandfather live?' I asked.

Matteo didn't even glance up from his phone as he answered. 'On an estate on the outskirts of Athens. We'll be there shortly.'

I nodded, too miserable to try to make conversation. It seemed every time we made some progress in our relationship we were knocked back again. Could I keep living this way? Did I have any choice?

Twenty minutes later we pulled up on the circular drive in front of an imposing and austere villa, its windows shuttered tight. I'd never thought a house could look unfriendly, but this one did.

A dour-faced butler met us at the door, Matteo striding ahead while I instinctively lagged behind, unsure where my place was in this fractured drama.

'Mr Arides wishes to see both of you immediately,' the butler said in Greek.

'Immediately?' Matteo glowered. 'He calls, I jump?'

'He says it is urgent, sir.'

'*I'll* decide what's urgent. My wife and I would like to wash off the dust of travel. We've been in the air for fourteen hours.'

Matteo brushed past the man and I had no choice but to follow.

Up in a soberly decorated guest room Matteo stripped off his suit and headed to the shower without so much as speaking to me. I sank onto a sofa and stared around miserably, unsure whether to rally or cut my losses.

Are you really going to chicken out as soon as things get tough? Are you just going to slink away? My inner optimist was a persistent whisper. *Is that the kind of wife you want to be?*

No, it most certainly wasn't—yet something in me shrank to a shrivelled bit of nothing when Matteo adopted that remote, imperious attitude. It felt like a twenty-foot-high stone wall, or perhaps an electric fence.

Do not touch. Do not even approach.

Still, I told myself, *I would try.* For the sake of what I hoped we both felt, I had to try.

I heard the shower being turned off and a few minutes later Matteo came into the room, wearing nothing but a towel loosely about his hips. I swallowed hard at the sight of him, all chiselled muscle and hard angles, but his eyes were like steel.

A mere day ago he would have favoured me with a sleepy smile and then walked slowly over to me, dropping the towel as he went. We would have fallen onto the bed in a tangle of limbs and made love with leisurely enjoyment until the sun faded in the sky and we fell asleep in each other's arms.

Now Matteo turned away from me as he dropped the towel and unzipped his suitcase, pulling out fresh clothes.

'Matteo, will you please talk to me?' I asked, my voice wavering too much for my liking.

'There's nothing to say.' He pulled on a pair of boxer briefs and reached for a shirt.

'Ever since you received that telegram it's as if you're a different person.'

'No, I'm not.' His voice lashed out, striking me with what felt like a physical blow. 'I'm exactly the same.'

It sounded like a warning.

Still, I tried not to panic. Not to give in to my ever-present fear. Because I was stronger and smarter than that.

But not strong or smart enough to keep from

falling in love with a man who does not feel the same way about you.

No, I wasn't going to think like that. Not yet, anyway. Not until I had to.

'What's going on?' I asked, trying for a friendly and reasonable tone. 'Why do you think your grandfather called you so urgently?'

'Because he can.' One dark eyebrow arched as he buttoned his shirt and selected a tie.

'But *why* can he?' I pressed. 'Is it something to do with the shares?' I hesitated, unsure if I was wading into too-deep water…if I'd drown. 'It almost seems as if he has some hold over you.'

'Don't be so utterly ridiculous,' Matteo snapped. 'Of course he doesn't.' He pulled on a suit jacket and started from the room. 'I don't know how long I'll be. Don't wait up.'

'I thought he wanted to see both of us—'

'He'll have to make do with me.'

And with that he closed the door behind him, one note away from a slam.

I sank back onto the sofa, deflated, defeated. That had gone well. *Not.* I was at an impasse, but I told myself to be patient. Matteo was understandably tense at seeing his grandfather again. I could appreciate that. But his own emotions about that meeting did not have to play to my insecurities and fears. I couldn't let them.

Still, as the hours passed, I knew that was exactly what was happening.

I strode towards my grandfather's study, hating everything about this situation. Hating myself.

Daisy's words were a mocking refrain in my mind: *It almost seems as if he has some hold over you.*

Even she, after such a short amount of time, could see my weakness. Could sense that after thirty-six years of abuse and insult at the hands of a bitter old man I still came running. Still came begging, like a dog waiting to be kicked.

It was an instinct that I couldn't seem to get rid of, no matter how hard I tried. Oh, it wasn't as painfully obvious as it had been when I was a child—working as hard as I could to impress him, waiting for his infrequent visits in the utterly vain and pointless hope that one day, *one day*, I'd do and be enough. Show him I was worthy of love, or at least some affection.

He never gave me any.

In my university days and early adulthood my method for impressing him changed, and I pursued a self-destructive course in a bid to get his attention, all the while pretending I didn't care. I caroused and partied and picked up women, had my exploits splashed across the tabloids, knowing my grandfather would hate my playboy ways, so like his own son's, and telling myself I didn't care in the least.

I had him over a barrel; he had to give me control of his company because not only was there no one else to give it to, but quite simply I was the best. I'd yanked a failing business out of redlining mediocrity and made it the most powerful hotel empire in the world. Bastian Arides needed me, whether he wanted to or not—and he definitely did not.

But this time, I told myself as I stood outside his study door, I would *not* look for his approval. I would not seek to aggravate him either; that would be simply another attention grab. No, I would be completely indifferent. Whatever he wanted, I wouldn't care. I didn't care.

Because he *didn't* have a hold over me. Even if this house was filled with ghosts and memories; even if I could practically feel Eleni's pinching of my ear as she marched me to this very room. No, now I was going to be different.

I rapped once on the door and then strode in, without waiting for his word.

Bastian Arides was not standing behind his desk, the imposing and stern-faced giant of my childhood days. No, he was huddled in a rocking chair by a gas fire, even though the day was warm. He looked gaunt, almost skeletal, and there was a yellowish cast to his drawn and wrinkled face.

'Matteo.'

He said my name with resigned finality. I nodded my greeting and waited, not deigning to reply.

'Thank you for coming.'

'Now, that *is* surprising,' I couldn't keep from drawling. 'A word of thanks?'

I'd worked myself to the very bone saving his company, and he'd never once said a word to me. He'd only tolerated my presence as if I were a bad smell in the room and he had to put up with it.

'I realise my request might have seemed demanding—'

'*Might* have?' I couldn't keep myself from interjecting. My determination to remain coolly indifferent was failing at the first post. This man brought out the worst in me—the neediest and the angriest.

'It did,' he amended in an unusual about-face. 'But the truth is, Matteo, I don't know how much time I have left. The doctor has given me days.'

'Days?' I stared at him in disbelief. 'Four months ago you were in remission.'

'Sometimes, especially at my age, remission doesn't last very long.'

He smiled sadly, but I was unmoved. Did he actually think I was going to grieve for him?

'I don't see what any of this has to do with me,' I said. 'We've had little to do with one another over the years. As little as possible.'

'I know that, and I want to rectify it.'

'Rectify it?' I let out a hard laugh. 'Are you starting to regret your life now that you're about to shuffle off this mortal coil?'

Bastian Arides pressed his lips together and looked away. 'Something like that.'

Something in me hardened, and then crystallised. I finally had my grandfather where I'd always wanted him—and yet I found I didn't want it at all. Certainly not like this, begrudging and almost angry. What was he afraid of? Judgement? A weighing of the scales? He wanted absolution, but I knew in that moment that he wouldn't get it from me.

'Sorry, old man,' I drawled coldly. 'If you're looking for some kind of atonement to send you singing into the afterlife, forget it.'

His face twisted in a grimace of acknowledgement. 'I know it is much to ask.'

'That's an understatement.' I gave him a long, hard stare. 'What is this *really* about? I can't believe that an old tyrant like you would quake at the thought of what happens after you die.'

'It's not so much the after,' he answered quietly, 'as the now.'

I frowned, folding my arms impatiently. 'What is that supposed to mean?'

'Knowing death is near makes one look back on one's life. See things more clearly.'

'And what *do* you see so clearly?' I couldn't keep the scorn from my voice; I didn't even try.

Bastian Arides hesitated, and I saw—felt—the reluctance in him, seeping from every pore. Hard, proud man that he was, he didn't want to admit anything to me. If he wanted my forgiveness it was for his sake, not mine. He still didn't care a whit about me.

'I've come to see that I was too hard on you,' he said at last.

I let out a laugh that was a bit too wild. 'Too hard on me? That's all you've got? And you want my forgiveness?'

'I'm dying, Matteo—'

'And I'll see you in hell.'

Without another word I turned and walked out, slamming the door behind me.

Fury poured through me in a scalding acid rush, making my fists clench and my heart thud.

How dared he? How dared he?

After all this time, after all the abuse, he thought I'd take his *I suppose I have to say sorry* attitude and be *thankful*? Be cringingly, pathetically grateful? And the hell of it was he hadn't even *said* sorry.

I couldn't go back and face Daisy; I didn't even want to. I pictured her face when we'd spoken earlier, soft and sad in confusion, wanting to help, wanting me to let her in, and I both despaired and raged because of it.

No, I couldn't let her in. I wouldn't. Because the horrible, humiliating truth was part of me wanted to accept Bastian Arides's pathetic offer. Part of me wanted to crawl right up to him and thank him for finally taking the time to so much as look at me.

And I hated that more than I'd hated anything else—except Daisy knowing.

So I strode away from the house, down through the gardens, just needing to *move*—because if I didn't I was afraid of what I might do.

'Matteo.'

I whirled around to see Daisy at the edge of the lawn; she must have followed me. 'Don't,' I warned her. 'Just don't.'

'Don't what?' she asked softly.

Don't ask me what's wrong. Don't look at me like that, as if I'm breaking your heart when it's mine that's in agony. Don't love me, because I don't think I can bear it.

'Just don't.'

She stared at me for a moment, and then she started forward. 'Matteo, I want to help. I want to be with you—'

'Don't.'

The word came out close to a roar, and I turned away from her, away from all of it, striding back to the house and slamming the door, as if I could actually outrun the demons that tormented me.

CHAPTER FIFTEEN

'MAY I SPEAK with you for a moment?'

Startled, I turned to see an elderly man who could only be Matteo's grandfather standing in the doorway of the library, where I'd been waiting out a miserable morning. After I'd seen Matteo in the garden he'd disappeared for the rest of the day, and he hadn't come to our bedroom—our bed—that night. I hadn't seen him this morning either, and I was fighting off a dragging sense of despair.

Why was he pushing me away so hard? When would he stop?

'Yes, of course.'

I rose from my seat, but Bastian Arides waved me back down as he shuffled slowly into the room.

'As you can see, I'm not very well.' He sat down in the chair opposite me with a quiet groan of relief.

'I'm sorry...'

'It happens to us all. I'm an old man. I've lived my life, for better or for worse.' He eyed me with weary appraisal. 'So you are the woman my grandson married?'

I nodded, unsure how to respond, having no idea what this man thought of me. Looking at him now, I thought he didn't seem the terrible tyrant Matteo had painted such a bleak picture of. He looked nothing more than an old man—a very ill old man.

'I'm dying,' he said abruptly, as if he sensed my thoughts. 'Did Matteo tell you?'

'I haven't seen him since yesterday afternoon,' I admitted.

'Ah. He is very angry with me, I'm afraid.'

'Why?'

Bastian gave a little shrug. 'Because I asked him to forgive me, I suppose.'

I started at that, because that was the last thing I'd expected. 'He's angry with you because you want to make amends?'

'It is not always easy to let go of our grievances.'

'Yes, but…' He was *dying*. And, however much Matteo hated his grandfather, here was a chance to right old wrongs, heal old wounds. How could he reject it?

'Matteo is a very proud man,' Bastian said slowly. 'He has worked hard for what he has. He saved Arides Enterprises, did you know that?'

'Sort of...'

I gazed at him cautiously. Matteo had told me the empire had been in trouble when he'd come in and risked everything on its fledgling luxury hotel market. His gamble had paid off.

'Well, he did. I was not as good a businessman as he was. I didn't like to take risks. And his father...' Bastian sighed. 'His father had no head for it at all. As well as no interest.'

'Matteo said something of that to me.'

'Matteo was my saviour,' he stated starkly. 'And I confess I hated that. I didn't want to be saved—and certainly not by a child I hadn't even wanted to raise.'

I recoiled a little at his honest words. 'Why blame Matteo for the circumstances of his birth?' I asked.

'I didn't—not precisely. It was simply that he was too painful a reminder of my daughter-in-law's death. I loved her, you see, and when she died I blamed Matteo.'

I must have looked shocked because Bastian hastened to clarify.

'I loved her as a daughter. She was so gentle, so kind. And my son treated her dreadfully—gambling, drinking, having affairs. Taking Matteo in was an act of kindness on her part, but it was one that killed her, and I blamed Matteo for that. He reminded me of his father, who had been such a disappointment. I suppose it all became mixed up in my mind…and Matteo was an easy target.' He smiled sadly. 'He made it difficult for me in any case…always acting out. But I admit I made very little effort.'

'How did taking in Matteo kill her?' I asked.

'She wasn't strong physically or emotionally… and Andreas's birth—do you know about Andreas?'

I nodded.

'Poor, dear Andreas. His birth affected her badly. She never really recovered. Taking Matteo in…that was difficult for her, both emotionally and physically. And then to try to look after two baby boys, knowing one was the child of her husband's whore…'

'His mother wasn't a whore. And how can taking care of a couple of children kill anyone? She must have had help…?'

'Yes, there was a nanny. But Marina didn't like to leave the care of the boys to her. She wanted them to grow up as brothers.' His face twisted. 'Something *I* couldn't stand.'

I shook my head slowly, both saddened and repulsed by his plain speaking. He was a hard man, but he was also a broken one. 'So how did she die?'

He paused, and then said starkly, 'She killed herself. An overdose. We didn't let the news out. I don't think Matteo even knows.'

'And you blamed Matteo for it?' I surmised. Poor Matteo. Poor Marina.

'Yes, I did. I know it isn't logical, but it was the reaction of a grief-stricken man. I didn't want him in my home, although I knew I had a responsibility towards him. I couldn't bear it after the disappointment of my son, the death of my daughter-in-law… I sent him away with the nanny. I provided for him. I made sure he had adequate food and clothing, education and opportunity.'

'But not the same as Andreas.'

'No—and why should he have?' Bastian challenged me. 'Perhaps in America things are done differently, but here birth and family matter. I did my duty by Matteo, but he never saw that.'

I shook my head. As much as Bastian Arides's broken state touched me, Matteo's sad childhood moved me more. 'Perhaps because you ignored and insulted him.'

'Ignoring him was the best I could do. He reminded me of all I'd lost. Seeing him was too painful. It made me too angry.' He bowed his head. 'I admit it makes me weak, but it is the truth nonetheless. And in any case Matteo was not an easy person to love or even to be around. He was always lashing out, trying to irritate me or anger me. He was suspended from school six times, and was finally expelled. Did he tell you that?'

I shook my head, and Bastian continued.

'In his teens he started with the drinking and the women, knowing those had been his father's vices. He taunted me with them, was as public as possible, knowing it would bring me shame. I don't suppose he told you that, either?'

'Not precisely, but I know he's had a reckless past. You're the one assigning motives.'

Bastian let out a weary sigh, his thin shoul-

ders slumping. 'I know I sound as if I'm justifying myself, and perhaps I am. But I want to
make amends now. My son died not knowing
my forgiveness, and my daughter-in-law slipped
away from this world like a shadow, without a
word of farewell. My own wife died many years
ago, from cancer. I want to leave this world in
peace, knowing I have done my utmost to recon-
cile with those I've hurt because I wasn't strong
enough to love them.'

My throat tightened at the emotion in his face
and in his voice. No matter what Bastian Arides
had or hadn't done in his life, he was at the end
of it now, and I couldn't help but feel a grudg-
ing compassion for him. 'And you told Matteo
all of this?'

'Yes, but he wasn't having any of it. He told
me he'd see me in hell. I suppose that is where
I'll be going.'

'Don't,' I implored. He sounded so despairing.
'Give him time. He'll see sense, I'm sure. You
can't expect him to change so quickly—'

'I don't think he will, my dear. I think, perhaps, it is too late. Too late for Matteo to forgive
or to change—at least in regard to me.'

His words echoed hollowly in me, because it

was what I feared as well. *Too late.* It was too late for Bastian…and too late for us.

'Will you talk to him for me?' Bastian asked, leaning forward to touch my hand. 'He might listen to you.'

'I'll try, although I'm not sure he will.'

Bastian gave a small smile. 'I have seen photographs of the two of you in the press. He looks like a man in love.'

I let out a little hollow laugh, even as his words offered me a faint flicker of hope. 'I'll do my best,' I promised, both for Bastian's sake and my own.

If Matteo couldn't forgive a dying man, what hope could there be for us to have a truly loving relationship?

I spent the rest of the day in a ferment of sorrowful anxiety, wondering when I'd see Matteo again and if I'd have the courage to speak to him when I did. He'd been like a stranger since we'd been in Athens. I felt as if I didn't know him at all…and I was afraid that I didn't.

Finally, that evening, he appeared in our bedroom. I'd spent the day alone, eating in my room, feeling like a prisoner in this lonely old house. Part of me longed to return to Amanos, to the comfort of friends and work and a busy, happy life, without all the emotional highs and lows I'd been see-sawing between over these last few weeks.

Matteo didn't say anything when he caught sight of me curled up in a chair by the window, the shutters open to the velvety evening. It was properly spring now, so even the night air was warm. Inside our room, though, it felt cold. Far too cold.

'Where have you been, Matteo?' I tried my best to sound merely curious and not accusing. 'I haven't seen you all day.'

'I've been busy,' he returned shortly, and then disappeared into the bathroom. A few minutes later the shower started running.

I took a deep breath, willing myself to be strong enough for the conversation ahead… Whatever it took. Whatever it cost.

After what felt like an endless twenty minutes, and yet was all too short a time, Matteo emerged from the bathroom. He didn't look at me as he pulled on a pair of trousers and a casual polo shirt.

'Matteo…'

My voice wobbled and I almost gave up right

then and there. His back was to me, and everything about him prickled with defensiveness and even irritation. He did not want to have this or any conversation with me.

Then I remembered what kind of wife I wanted to be. How I wasn't going to give up on us at the first, admittedly high hurdle. So I took a deep breath and, feeling as if I were throwing myself off a cliff, plunged ahead.

'We need to talk.'

I tensed where I stood, everything in me resisting. Of course Daisy wanted us to talk. She wanted to *know*. I'd spent the last day and a half keeping out of her way and keeping my head down, working. When I focused on business it blotted out all the other thoughts and memories clamouring in my brain. Almost.

But now, as much as I wanted to dismiss her and keep on with work because it offered me salvation, I knew I couldn't. This reckoning had to come at some point. It might as well be now.

I turned around to face her and folded my arms. 'Fine. Let's talk.'

She looked at me uncertainly, clearly taking in

my aggressive stance. 'Your grandfather spoke to me this morning,' she said after a moment.

I jerked back. 'That was manipulative—even for the old bastard.'

'Matteo, he wants your forgiveness—'

I could hardly believe that she was taking his side, that this conversation was going to be about *him*. 'He's not going to get it. I don't want to discuss it, Daisy—and, frankly, it has nothing to do with you.'

She blinked, her eyes full of hurt. 'Do you really mean that?'

'I've told you my history with that man. It doesn't give you the right to interfere.'

Her hand came up to her throat. 'Interfering? Is that what you think I'm doing?'

'In this? Yes.' I stared at her flatly, refusing to be moved one inch. One iota.

Daisy drew a shaky breath. 'I know he hurt you...' she began.

I made a scoffing sound. 'You have no idea—and I really don't want your pity. I certainly didn't ask for it. Just drop it, Daisy. It has absolutely nothing to do with you.'

'He wants your forgiveness, Matteo,' she repeated doggedly, and for once I didn't like that determined tilt of her chin. 'Can't you respect that? Honour it?'

'No, as a matter of fact, I can't.'

'He can't help it that he wasn't strong enough to love you the way he should have—'

'Is *that* what he told you? What a crock of—'

'He's *dying*—'

'He really gave you the full sob story, didn't he? He's been "dying" for three years.'

Daisy pressed her lips together. 'You just have to look at him to know this really is it, Matteo—'

'Then fine. This is it. Good riddance, I say.'

I met her shocked gaze with a flinty one of my own. If Daisy couldn't accept this, if she couldn't back down, then fine. So be it.

'How can you be so cruel?' she asked in a low voice. 'To a dying man?'

I opened my mouth to ask her if she knew what he'd done, what he was capable of. But then I didn't. Because I already knew the answer. She didn't know because I hadn't wanted to tell her. And I wasn't going to tell her now because it was suddenly, glaringly obvious what was really going on here.

We were finished.

The last two weeks we'd been play-acting at

marriage, even at being in love, but for all my talk of a real marriage it wasn't real at all. *This* was.

'Daisy, I'm afraid I'm not the man you seem to persist in thinking I am. Some gentle, tender, tortured soul who will take his dying grandfather in his arms and pat his fevered brow, all the while assuring him of my love and good will.' I locked on her gaze unflinchingly. 'I'm not that man at all.'

'You're a good man, Matteo.'

She sounded uncertain, and that made me ache, which only made me more determined to do the one thing I could.

'I think we most likely have a difference of opinion when it comes to what we think a good man is. If a good man to you is someone who forgives and loves easily, then I'm afraid you're sadly mistaken. *Deluded.*'

She jerked back at that word, and something flashed across her face that looked deeper than hurt, worse than fear.

'I'm not that man, Daisy. I was never that man. I warned you at the start. I made it quite clear. I am not interested in the illusion of love.'

'Do you really think it's an illusion,' she whispered, 'or are you just afraid of it?'

I stilled at that, because she had pierced to the very heart of the matter and in that moment I hated her for it.

'I am not afraid,' I snarled. 'And if you can't agree to the terms of this marriage that I set out at the beginning, then—' I broke off, even now not wanting to deliver the final blow and fell her. Fell our chance at happiness. Because I had been happy these last few weeks. Happier than I'd ever been in my life.

But what was a little happiness?

'Then what?' Daisy whispered. Her face was pale, her lips bloodless. 'Just what is your ultimatum?'

'Then we won't have much longer to finish out this convenient marriage,' I said, the words falling into the stillness like pebbles being dropped down a well. 'My grandfather has only a few more weeks to live, if that.'

She flinched, but still held my gaze. 'We can't get an annulment any more. Are you asking for a divorce?'

Was she trying to push me into one—or into

some pointless declaration? Either way, I would not be manipulated.

'We can sort the details out later. There's also the matter of a potential pregnancy,' I reminded her. 'I will not divorce the mother of my child.'

'Well, you can rest easy there,' she answered, a ragged note entering her voice. 'Because I'm not pregnant. I got my period this morning.'

I ignored the wave of disappointment that caused to crash over me. It was better this way.

'So I'll go, then?'

She rose from her seat, all wounded dignity and barely-there pride. *That chin.*

'Back to Amanos?'

I stood there, howling inside, and part of me—a very large part—even now wanted to take it all back. To take her into my arms and beg her to stay, to bear with me, because I was honestly trying and everything in me was raw with grief and rage.

But I couldn't do it. I couldn't make myself that weak, that vulnerable. I couldn't bear to see the pity in her eyes, to feel the soft touch of her compassion. And I couldn't do as she asked and forgive my grandfather.

So I said nothing, and after an endless damning silence Daisy slowly nodded, the movement unbearably final.

It wasn't until she'd walked out of the room in the wake of my silence that I realised *this* was the weakest and most fearful I'd been yet—because I'd let her go.

CHAPTER SIXTEEN

'MATTY!'

I smiled at my brother even as everything in me ached. It had been twenty-four hours since Daisy had left for Amanos, and it had been the longest and most awful day of my life. The only bright light was the hours I'd spent with Andreas.

I knew I didn't see him enough. Since his injury Andreas had lived on the top floor of my grandfather's house, in a set of purpose-made rooms, with a full-time carer. He was happy that way, preferring routine to change, and he had all he could wish for—toys, books, a TV with endless DVDs... Everything a man with the mind of an eight-year-old could wish for.

What he didn't have was any attention or notice from his grandfather.

Spending time with him was simple for me. Before his accident Andreas and I had rubbed along together warily, during our infrequent times together, but since his injury we'd become close, because everything had become so wonderfully uncomplicated.

Now I smiled and sat down across from him on the floor, where he was building a huge construction out of plastic building bricks.

'What's this, then?' I asked, and Andreas proceeded to tell me about the city he was building in all its childish complexity.

After about fifteen minutes of happily chatting away, he looked up at me, blinking slowly. 'Matty, why are you sad?'

'Sad?' I tried to smile, but it wouldn't come this time. 'Why do you think I'm sad?'

'I can tell. You look like Pappous when he sees me. Always sad.'

I flinched at this, because I hated the thought of Andreas suffering under the weight of Bastian Arides's disappointment. The precious grandson he'd practically revered had become an embarrassing and unwanted pariah, and it had been that, along with his treatment of me, that had made me realise what an illusion love was.

But I was not afraid of it. No matter what Daisy said.

'Don't be sad,' Andreas implored. 'Play with me.'

'I'm always happy to play with you, Andreas.'

I reached over and picked up a brick. 'Where does this go?'

'Over here.'

For a few minutes we both concentrated on constructing his city, and it almost felt peaceful. The ache of losing Daisy was still intensely painful, but at least I could pretend to forget it for a little while.

A sound at the door had us both looking up, and I stiffened in surprise at the sight of my grandfather.

'Pappous!' Andreas exclaimed, seeming genuinely happy to see the old man.

I gave him a narrow-eyed look. We'd avoided each other for the last two days; the only reason I was still here was for Andreas.

I rose from where I was seated. 'I didn't think you came up here.'

'Pappous comes every day,' Andreas told me. 'He likes to play chess, but I'm not very good at it.'

'You're learning, dear boy,' Bastian said, and something in me flinched.

Was this new? Was he trying to win Andreas's forgiveness as well as my own? Manipulating a man with a child's mind and heart? It was a new low for him.

He turned to me, his expression both determined and bleak. 'Matteo,' he said. 'May we talk?'

'There's nothing more to say.'

'There is. I have something more to say, and I need you to hear it. After that you are free never to see or speak to me again, as you wish.'

'Never?' Andreas's voice wobbled and we both hastened to reassure him.

'He doesn't mean that, Andreas,' I said, although I knew he did. 'Keep building your city. I'll be back in a few moments.'

I strode out of the room, Bastian following me. Not wanting to leave Andreas for long, I stopped in the hallway, far enough away that he wouldn't overhear.

'What is it?'

Bastian glanced around, as if to object, but then he shrugged. 'I know I don't deserve a fair hearing from you. It was wrong of me to ask it of you before.'

'Is that all you have to say?'

'Matteo, is there anything I can do to help you to forgive me? I know I was wrong in the way I treated you. I justified it to myself because I was grieving the loss of Marina, your stepmother. I loved her like my own daughter—'

'What did that have to do with me?'

'I found it painful to know that you had been brought into the world, a healthy and hale boy, but she withered and then slipped away.'

'Still not my fault,' I gritted. I wasn't giving an inch.

'I admit I was unjust. I was angry, as well as ashamed that I had an illegitimate grandson— that it was known publicly—'

'That was your fault, not mine.'

'I didn't feel you deserved the same privilege or affection as Andreas. And you reminded me of your father, who was such a painful disappointment to me. I let it cloud my judgement. I admit that.'

'And has anything changed now?' I scoffed. 'Or are you just fearful because you face death?'

'I want to die in peace, yes,' he said slowly, swaying a bit where he stood.

He looked old and frail, as if a breath might blow him away, and I tried not to care. Tried not to admit to the grief inside me. Because there was no earthly reason to grieve for this man.

'I did provide for you, Matteo,' he added with a small, sad smile. 'Not in the same way as I did for Andreas, I know, but I tried to do my duty.'

'Your *duty*?' I sneered. 'Was starving me your duty? Was slapping my face for just sitting down your duty? Or locking me in a cupboard?' The words burst out of me, decades old, full of pain.

Bastian stared at me for a long moment. 'What…what are you talking about?'

'You *know* what I'm talking about. Eleni—the nanny you hired to look after me. She made it very clear what her orders were, how she was to treat the worthless bastard you'd been saddled with.'

Slowly Bastian shook his head. 'Matteo, I admit I did not treat you fairly. I was harsh and unloving. But I didn't know about those things. I certainly didn't sanction them.'

For a second, no more, I wavered. But then, 'Yes, you did. She told me. And in any case, when I did see you, you were completely dismissive. Nothing I did was ever good enough. No matter how hard I worked or tried, you were unimpressed. Always ignoring me or insulting me, even after you had to make me your heir.'

'Yes,' Bastian agreed heavily. 'I admit to

all that. I was not the man I wish I could have been. I wasn't strong enough. I resented having to need you. I felt it should have been you, not Andreas…' He shook his head. 'It was wrong—all of it—I see that now. But I never would have countenanced such abuse. Please believe that at least, even if you cannot forgive me.'

I shook my head. I didn't know what to believe. For over thirty-five years the bedrock of my life—of my whole being—had been my grandfather's harsh treatment of me. It had taught me everything: never to be vulnerable, never to show fear, never to trust love. They were the staples of my soul, and now they felt like so much dross. I couldn't let go of them just like that. If I did, I didn't know who I'd be.

A man who could love. Who could let himself be loved.

'What about Andreas?' I demanded.

Bastian looked startled. 'What about him?'

'After his accident you ignored him, as well. You never visited him. You turned your love off like it was a tap.'

'I admit I avoided him for several years after the accident. It was too painful for me to see him like that, and when I did see him he became distressed, which made it even worse. But I've been visiting him for years, Matteo. Decades. Every day, just as he said. I still love him. I'll always love him.'

'And me?' I found myself saying, even as I hated the words, the exposing and needy nature of the question.

'I wish I could have loved you as a child,' Bastian said slowly. 'You were deserving of it. But when you rebelled as a teenager it cemented my anger and bitterness. I shouldn't have let it.'

I waited, my jaw tight, everything in me tensed and poised—for what?

'And now...' Bastian continued, choosing each word with painful care, his gaze steady on me. 'Now I see a man who has an indomitable will, a fearless work ethic, and a loyalty to those he loves. You have always made time for Andreas—'

'He's my brother.'

'And your wife.'

I let out a sharp laugh. 'How little you know! I didn't see her once for the first three years of our marriage.'

And I might never see her again.

'But now you love her,' Bastian stated—a

fact, a truth. 'I see it in your eyes…in every-thing about you. And I know you are a man who fights for what he wants. Who he loves.'

He paused, and then said the words I'd waited my whole life to hear.

'I love you, Matteo. I don't expect you to be-lieve it, or even to care, but I do love you like a son. I only wish I had earlier, and that I'd been able to show it.'

I shook my head, denying it even as tears started in my eyes. My grandfather gave me a look full of sorrow and grief—and love. I saw it in his eyes for the first time.

'I'm sorry, son,' he said.

'Daisy, your head is in the sky again.'

Maria shook her finger at me, laughing, and I tried for a smile even though I felt leaden inside.

'The clouds,' I reminded her. 'And I'm sorry. I'm a bit distracted.'

I'd been back in Amanos for two days, but I felt like the walking wounded. The walking dead. Because something had died inside me when Matteo had let me walk away. And I'd done it—high-tailing it when it got hard, even though I'd told myself I wouldn't. I was as much a coward as he was—if he even *was* a coward. Perhaps he wasn't scared of love as I'd suggested. Perhaps he really didn't believe in it—or feel it.

'What is distracting you?' Maria asked. 'The so very handsome Kyrie Dias?'

I hadn't told Maria or anyone about what had happened between Matteo and me, although most of the villagers had seen at least some of the photos that had appeared in the tabloids and on the online gossip sites. They could guess, although no one could possibly know how badly it had all ended.

'Daisy.' Maria placed a hand on my shoulder, her eyes filled with concern. 'What is it? What's wrong?'

And then, to both my embarrassment and my relief, I burst into tears. I ended up telling her the whole sorry story, from beginning to end, as the tears kept trickling down my face.

'He doesn't love me, Maria,' I finished as I blew my nose. 'I gambled everything on the hope that he would learn to, with time—and he didn't. I don't think he's capable of it.'

Maria patted my shoulder in sympathy and then sat back with a loud sigh. 'I don't who is *perissotero* stupid—you or him.'

'What?' I managed an outraged laugh. 'What do you mean?'

'You are in love with him, Daisy, and he is in love with you. To me it is obvious.'

'You weren't there…'

'*Pfft.* I don't need to have been there. A man does not act like Kyrie Dias did when he is indifferent. So much emotion…he is in love.'

I stared at her disbelievingly. 'Maria, he was so hard, so *cruel*—'

'Did you expect him to forgive his grandfather like that?' She snapped her fingers. 'Daisy, the man suffered under his hand for many, many years. Forgiveness, it is—what do you say?—a process. It is not an instant.'

I stared at her, realisation slowly dawning like a fog lifting. 'Do you think…do you think I demanded too much, asking him to forgive his grandfather?'

'Yes—and he pushed you away too hard because he was angry and grieving, even if he did not show it.' She paused, her expression reflective. 'My husband Antonio's mother, she was a cruel woman. Harsh and unloving. But when she died, he grieved. So much. Because something was lost even though he had not loved her. The hope of love one day.'

'I didn't think of that.'

And it was the hope of love that I had been yearning for, and then grieving for. My own desires and fears had blinded me to whatever Matteo had been feeling.

'I think I have been stupid,' I said with a sad smile. 'But it's too late now. Matteo...he was so final, Maria. He more or less said he wanted a divorce.'

'More or less?' She raised her eyebrows, her smile almost smug. 'A bit less, I think.'

'I don't know...'

'You could find him.'

I thought of how I'd marched into that ballroom, all terrified determination, having no idea what I was getting into. Could I do it again? Did I dare?

'I don't know where he is.'

'Then find out.'

All day long I dithered, caught between fear and a wild, desperate hope. But when I plucked up the courage to search the gossip sites for any titbit about where Matteo was, I came up empty. Determined, I called the head office of Arides

Enterprises in Athens, only to be told he had left that morning and would not be back for at least a week.

Where had he gone? And was I brave enough to find him?

That evening, as I sat outside on the terrace, trying to enjoy the rays of the setting sun and not to feel miserable, the distant whirring of a helicopter had me sitting up straight. Hope flared, hard and bright, inside me.

Could it be...?

I scrambled to the terrace wall, craning my head to catch sight of the helicopter, praying it wasn't a search and rescue one. When it came into view, the *A* and the *E* both visible, I let out a whoop of joy—followed by a tremor of pure terror. What if he was coming to tell me he did indeed want a divorce?

At least I'd have a chance to talk to him, I told myself. Fight for him. For *us*.

It seemed to take an age, but in reality I had only a few minutes to wait for the helicopter to land, for Matteo to emerge. I watched from the window as he strode towards the house, looking far too grimly determined. Then I decided I wasn't going to wait—I was going to fight.

I threw open the door and ran outside, heedless of my bare feet, my wild look.

'Matteo—'

He stopped, holding up one hand. 'Don't,' he said, just as he had before.

My heart plummeted like a stone inside me.

'Don't say anything.'

'But—'

'I need to speak first.'

Dumbly, I nodded, having no idea what to expect, how much to hope.

'Daisy, I love you.'

My mouth dropped open as incredulous joy unfurled through me in a sweet, warm rush of feeling.

'I've been fighting it for a while now, because you were right—I *am* afraid of it. I convinced myself it was an illusion because that was far easier and, I thought, far braver than admitting my fear.'

'What happened?' I whispered. 'What made you…change your mind?'

'I spoke to my grandfather again. He was honest with me—more honest than he's ever been before. And I was honest with him.' He let out a ragged, pent-up breath. 'There were things he